Am I Blue?

Coming Out from the Silence

Am I Blue?

Coming Out
from the Silence

edited by Marion Dane Bauer

HarperCollins*Publishers*

*For all young people in
their search for themselves*

CONTENTS

INTRODUCTION

*T*en years ago, an anthology of short stories dealing with gay and lesbian themes probably would not have been considered by any major young adult publisher. It is my dream that ten years from now such an anthology will not be needed, that gay and lesbian characters will be as integrated into juvenile literature as they are in life. Until that day comes, however, the fifteen authors contributing to this collection and I make this heartfelt offering.

One out of ten teenagers attempts suicide. One out of three of those does so because of concern about being homosexual. That means that in every statistical classroom across the country there is one young person in danger of dying for lack of information and support concerning his or her sexuality. The intention of this anthology is to tell challenging, honest, affecting stories that will open a window for all who seek to understand themselves or others.

A good friend of mine once said, "I have never

met a bigot who was a reader as a child," and it is something I believe as well. The power of fiction is that it gives us, as readers, the opportunity to move inside another human being, to look out through that person's eyes, hear with her ears, think with his thoughts, feel with her feelings. It is the only form of art which can accomplish that feat so deeply, so completely. And thus it is the perfect bridge for helping us come to know the other—the other inside as well as outside ourselves.

There is a well-intended prejudice abroad today, spoken loudly and persistently, that no one can write about those who stand outside of his or her own culture. And it is certainly true that fiction writers of the majority culture, especially those writing for young people, have too often sailed into territory where their understanding was inadequate for the stories they chose to tell. However, writing fiction is an act of informed imagination, and no one has a right to judge the manner in which a writer's information is received . . . only the final product.

Gay men and lesbians have their own culture in the late twentieth century. Some of the writers in this anthology come to their stories from within that culture; others have approached it from the outside with openness and compassion . . . and a willingness to learn. All have written with literary authority and psychological accuracy, which should go a long way toward dispelling that particular bias.

You will find this collection wide-ranging, from the delightful humor of Bruce Coville's title story, "Am I Blue?" and the irreverence (not religious but literary) of Gregory

Maguire's "The Honorary Shepherds" to the lyricism of Francesca Lia Block's "Winnie and Tommy" and the quiet honesty of M. E. Kerr's "We Might As Well All Be Strangers." Lois Lowry touches not just on the world of a gay father, but on the tender awkwardness of two teenage boys in a "male bonding" session. William Sleator explores another country; James Cross Giblin, another time; Jane Yolen, another world. All have brought a vital core of themselves to their stories, in addition to their very considerable skills as writers of literature for young people. Each story has touched my heart as an editor. I am confident that they will touch yours.

I thank all the authors who had the courage to take on this complex and, unfortunately, still-controversial topic. I thank, as well, the many writers who submitted stories to be considered for this collection, work that was passionate and thoughtful and intriguing, but which space would not allow me to use. And I thank David Gale for nurturing and supporting this idea from its first inception.

Royalties for this book are being shared with Parents, Families and Friends of Lesbians and Gays (P-FLAG) for their Respect All Youth Project, whose mission is to disseminate information about healthy sexuality to all youth. When you purchase this book, you are helping in their fine work.

AM I BLUE?

by Bruce Coville

for Pete

*I*t started the day Butch Carrigan decided I was interested in jumping his bones.

"You little fruit," he snarled. "I'll teach you to look at *me!*"

A moment or two later he had given me my lesson.

I was still lying facedown in the puddle into which Butch had slammed me as the culminating exercise of my learning experience when I heard a clear voice exclaim, "Oh, my dear! That *was* nasty. Are you all right, Vince?"

Turning my head to my left, I saw a pair of brown Docksiders, topped by khaki pants. Given the muddy condition of the sidewalks, pants and shoes were both ridiculously clean.

I rolled onto my side and looked up. The loafers belonged to a tall, slender man. He had dark hair, a neat mustache, and a sweater slung over his shoulders. He was kind of handsome—almost pretty. He wore a gold ring in his left ear. He looked to be about thirty.

"Who are you?" I asked suspiciously.

"Your fairy godfather. My name is Melvin. Come on, stand up and let's see if we can't do something with you."

"Are you making fun of me?" I asked. After Butch's last attack I had had about enough of people calling me a fruit for one day.

"Moi?" cried the man, arching his eyebrows and laying a hand on his chest. "Listen, honey, I have nothing but sympathy for you. I had to deal with my share of troglodytes when I was your age, and I *know* it's no fun. I'm here to help."

"What the hell are you talking about?"

"I told you, I'm your fairy godfather."

He waited for me to say something, but I just sat in the puddle, glaring at him. (It was uncomfortable, but I was already soaked right through my undershorts, so it didn't make that much difference.)

"You know," he said encouragingly. "Like in 'Cinderella'?"

"Go away and let me suffer in peace," I growled, splashing muddy water at him.

He flinched and frowned, but it was a reflex action; the water that struck his pants vanished without a trace.

I blinked, and splashed at him again, this time spattering a double handful of dirty water across his legs.

"Are you angry or just making a fashion statement?" he asked.

I felt a little chill. No spot of mud nor mark of moisture could be seen on the perfectly pressed khakis. "How did you do that?" I asked.

He just smiled and said, "Do you want your three wishes or not, Vincent?"

I climbed out of the puddle. "What's going on here?" I asked.

He made a *tsk*ing sound. "I think it's pretty obvious," he said, rolling his eyes. "Come on, let's go get a cup of coffee and talk. All your questions will be answered in good time."

The first question I thought of was "How much trouble is it going to give me to be seen with this guy?" With Butch and his crowd already calling me "faggot" and "fruit," walking around with a guy who moved the way Melvin did wasn't going to do anything to improve the situation.

The first question I actually *asked* was "Do you have to walk like that?"

"Like what?"

"You know," I said, blushing a little. "So swishy."

Melvin stopped. "Honey, I gave my life to be able to walk like this. Don't you dare try to stop me now."

"Don't call me honey!" I snapped.

He sighed and rolled his eyes toward the sky. "I can't say you didn't warn me," he said, clearly not speaking to me.

We went to a little cafe on Morton Street called Pete's. It's mostly frequented by kids from the university, but some of the high school kids hang out there as well, especially kids from the theater group.

"Not bad," said Melvin as we entered. "Brings back memories."

Things were slow, and we found a corner table where we could talk in private.

"Okay," I said, "what's going on?"

I won't relate the first part of the conversation, because you've probably read a lot of things like it before. I couldn't believe what he was saying was real, so I kept trying to figure out what this was really about—*Candid Camera*, an elaborate practical joke, that kind of thing . But after he instantly dried my puddle-soaked pants by snapping his fingers, I had to accept it: Whether or not he was actually my fairy godfather, this guy was doing real magic left and right.

"Okay, if you're real," I said, lifting my coffee (which had changed from plain coffee to Swiss double mocha *while* I was drinking it), "then tell me how come I never heard of fairy godfathers before."

"Because I'm the first."

"Care to explain that?"

"Certainly. Once you buy the farm, you get some choices on the other side. What kind of choices depends on the usual stuff—how good you've been and so on. Well, I was going up and not down, and it was pretty much expected that I would just opt to be an angel; tracking system, you know. But I said I didn't want to be anyone's guardian angel, I wanted to be a fairy godfather."

He took a sip of coffee and rolled his eyes. "Let me tell you, *that* caused a hullaballoo! But I said people had been calling me a fairy all my life, and now that I was dead, that was what I wanted to be. Then I told them that if they didn't let me be a fairy godfather, I was going to bring charges of sexism against

6

them. So they let me in. You're my first case."

"Does that have any significance?" I asked nervously.

"What do you mean?"

"Me being your first case. Does that mean I'm gay?"

I didn't mention that I had been trying to figure out the same thing myself for about a year now.

He got that look in his eye that meant he was about to make another wisecrack. But suddenly his face got serious. Voice soft, he said, "You may be, you may not. The point is, you're getting picked on because people *think* you are—which is why I've been sent to work with you. Gaybashing is a special issue for me."

"How come?"

"It's how I met my maker, so to speak. I was walking down the street one day last year, minding my own business, when three bruisers dragged me into an alley, shouting, 'We'll teach you, faggot!' They never did explain exactly what it was they were going to teach me. Last thing I remember from life on earth was coming face to face with a tire iron. Next thing I knew, I was knocking at the Pearly Gates."

We were both silent for a moment. Then he shrugged and took another sip of his coffee.

"You're taking this awfully casually," I said, still stunned by the awfulness of what he had told me.

"Honey, I did a lot of screaming and shouting while it was happening. Afterward too, for that matter. Didn't do me a bit of good—I was still dead. Once you've been on the other side for a while, you get a little more zen about this kind of thing."

"But don't you want to go get those guys or something?"

He shook his head. "I prefer reform to vengeance. Besides, it's against the rules. Why don't we just concentrate on your case for the time being."

"Okay, do I really get three wishes?"

"Sure do. Well, two, now."

"What do you mean?"

"You used up the first one on that coffee."

"I didn't tell you to change it into Swiss double mocha!" I yelped.

"You didn't have to. You wished for it."

"I'm glad I didn't wish I was dead!" I muttered.

"Oh!" he cried. "Getting personal, are we? Don't you think that remark was a little tasteless under the circumstances?"

"Are you here to help me or to drive me nuts?"

"It hurts me that you could even ask. Anyway, the three wishes are only part of the service, even though that's what people always focus on. I'm really here to watch over you, advise you, guide you, till we get things on track."

He leaned back in his chair, glanced around the room, then winked at a nice-looking college student sitting about five tables away from us.

"Will you stop that!" I hissed.

"What's the matter, afraid of guilt by association?"

"No, I'm afraid he'll come over here and beat us up. Only he probably can't beat you up, so he'll have to settle for me."

Melvin waved his hand. "I guarantee you he wasn't offended. He's one of the gang."

"What gang?"

Melvin pursed his lips and raised his eyebrows, as if he

couldn't believe I could be so dense.

I blinked. "How can you tell something like that just from looking at him?"

"Gaydar," said Melvin, stirring his coffee. "Automatic sensing system that lets you spot people of similar persuasion. A lot of gay guys have it to some degree or other. If it was more reliable, it would make life easier on us—"

I interrupted. "Speak for yourself."

Melvin sighed. "I wasn't necessarily including *you* in that particular 'us.' I was just pointing out that it's harder spotting potential partners when you're gay. If a guy asks a girl for a date, about the worst that can happen is that she laughs at him. If he asks another guy, he might get his face pounded in."

That thought had crossed my mind more than once as I was trying to figure myself out over the last year—and not only with regard to dating. I would have been happy just to have someone I felt safe *talking* to about this.

"Is this gaydar something you can learn?" I asked.

He furrowed his brow for a moment, then said, "I don't think so."

"It must be lonely," I muttered, more to myself than to him.

"It doesn't have to be," he replied sharply. "If gay people hadn't been forced to hide for so long, if we could just openly identify ourselves, there would be plenty of people you knew that you could ask for advice. Everybody knows gay people; they just think they don't."

"What do you mean?"

"Listen, honey, the world is crawling with faggots. But most of them are in hiding because they're afraid they'll get treated the way you did about an hour ago."

I took in my breath sharply. Melvin must have seen the look of shock on my face, because he looked puzzled for a moment. Then he laughed. "That word bother you?"

"I was taught that it was impolite."

"It is. But if you live in a world that keeps trying to grind you down, you either start thumbing your nose at it or end up very, very short. Taking back the language is one way to jam the grinder. My friends and I called each other 'faggot' and 'queer' for the same reason so many black folks call each other 'nigger'—to take the words away from the people who want to use them to hurt us."

His eyes went dreamy for a moment, as if he was looking at something far away, or deep inside. "I walk and talk the way I do because I'm not going to let anyone else define me. I can turn it off whenever I want, you know."

He moved in his seat. I couldn't begin to tell you exactly what changed, but he suddenly looked more masculine, less . . . swishy.

"How did you do that?" I asked.

"Protective coloration," he said with a smile. "You learn to use it to get along in the world if you want. Only I got sick of living in the box the world prescribed; it was far too small to hold me. So I knocked down a few walls."

"Yeah, and look what happened. You ended up dead."

"They do like to keep us down," he said, stirring his coffee. Suddenly he smiled and looked more like himself again. "Do you know the three great gay fantasies?" he asked.

"I don't think so," I said nervously.

He looked at me. "How old are you?"

"Sixteen."

"Skip the first two. You're too young. It was number three that I wanted to tell you about anyway. We used to imagine what it would be like if every gay person in the country turned blue for a day."

My eyes went wide. "Why?"

"So all the straights would have to stop imagining that they didn't know any gay people. They would find out that they had been surrounded by gays all the time, and survived the experience just fine, thank you. They'd have to face the fact that there are gay cops and gay farmers, gay teachers and gay soldiers, gay parents and gay kids. The hiding would finally have to stop."

He looked at me for a moment. "How would you like to have the sight?" he asked.

"What?"

"How would you like to have gaydar for a while? You might find it interesting."

"Does this count as a wish?" I asked suspiciously.

"No, it's education. Comes under a different category."

"All right," I said, feeling a little nervous.

"Close your eyes," said Melvin.

After I did as he requested, I felt him touch each of my eyelids lightly. My cheeks began to burn as I wondered if anyone else had seen.

"Okay," he said. "Open up, big boy, and see what the world is really like."

I opened my eyes and gasped.

11

About a third of the people in the cafe—including the guy Melvin had winked at—were blue. Some were bright blue, some were deep blue, some just had a bluish tint to them.

"Are you telling me all those people are gay?" I whispered.

"To some degree or other."

"But so many of them?"

"Well, this isn't a typical place," said Melvin. "You told me the theater crowd hangs around in here." He waved his hand grandly. "Groups like that tend to have a higher percentage of gay people, because we're so naturally artistic." He frowned. "Of course, some bozos take a fact like that and decide that *everyone* doing theater is gay. Remember, two thirds of the people you're seeing *aren't* blue."

"What about all the different shades?" I asked.

"It's an indicator of degree. The dark blues are pretty much exclusively queer, while the lighter ones are less committed— or maybe like you, trying to make up their minds. I set it up so that you'll see at least a hint of blue on anyone who has had a gay experience. Come on, let's go for a walk."

It was like seeing the world through new eyes. Most of the people looked just the same as always, of course. But Mr. Alwain, the fat guy who ran the grocery store, looked like a giant blueberry—which surprised me, because he was married and had three kids. On the other hand, Ms. Thorndyke, the librarian, who everyone *knew* was a lesbian, didn't have a trace of blue on her.

"Can't tell without the spell," said Melvin. "Straights are

helpless at it. They're always assuming someone is or isn't for all the wrong reasons."

We were in the library because Melvin wanted to show me some books. "Here, flip through this," he said, handing me a one-volume history of the world.

My bluevision worked on pictures, too!

"Julius Caesar?" I asked in astonishment.

"'Every woman's husband, every man's wife,'" said Melvin. "I met him at a party on the other side once. Nice guy." Flipping some more pages, he said, "Here, check this one out."

"Alexander the Great was a fairy!" I cried.

"Shhhhh!" hissed Melvin. "We're in a library!"

All right, I suppose you're wondering about me—as in, was I blue?

The answer is, slightly.

When I asked Melvin to explain, he said, "The Magic Eight Ball says, 'Signs Are Mixed.' In other words, you are one confused puppy. That's the way it is sometimes. You'll figure it out after a while."

Watching the news that night was a riot. My favorite network anchor was about the shade of a spring sky—pale blue, but very definite. So was the congressman he interviewed, who happened to be a notorious Republican homophobe.

"Hypocrite," I spat.

"What brought that on?" asked Dad.

"Oh, nothing," I said, trying to figure out whether I was

relieved or appalled by the slight tint of blue that covered his features.

Don't get the idea that everyone I saw was blue. It broke down pretty much the way the studies indicate—about one person in ten solid blue, and one out of every three or four with some degree of shading.

I did get a kick out of the three blue guys I spotted in the sports feature on the team favored to win the Superbowl.

But it was that congressman who stayed on my mind. I couldn't forget his hypocritical words about "the great crime of homosexuality" and "the gay threat to American youth." I was brushing my teeth when I figured out what I wanted to do.

"No," I whispered, staring at my bluish face in the mirror. "I couldn't."

For one thing, it would probably mean another beating from Butch Carrigan.

Yet if I did it, nothing would ever be the same.

Rinsing away the toothpaste foam, I whispered Melvin's name.

"At your service!" he said, shimmering into existence behind me. "Ooooh, what a tacky bathroom. Where was your mother brought up, in a Kmart?"

"Leave my mother out of this," I snapped. "I want to make my second wish."

"And it is?"

"Gay fantasy number three, coast to coast."

He looked at me for a second, then began to smile. "How's midnight for a starting point?"

"Twenty-four hours should do the trick, don't you think?"
I replied.

He rubbed his hands, chuckled, and disappeared.

I went to bed, but not to sleep. I kept thinking about what it
would mean when the rest of the world could see what I had
seen today.

I turned on my radio, planning to listen to the news every
hour. I had figured the first reports would come in on the
one-o'clock news, but I was wrong. It was about twelve thirty
when special bulletins started announcing a strange phenome-
non. By one o'clock every station I could pick up was on full
alert. Thanks to the wonders of modern communication, it
had become obvious in a matter of minutes that people were
turning blue from coast to coast.

It didn't take much longer for people to start figuring out
what the blue stood for. The reaction ranged from panic to
hysterical denial to dancing in the streets. National Public
Radio quickly summoned a panel of experts to discuss what
was going to happen when people had to go to work the next
day.

"Or school," I muttered to myself. Which was when I got
my next idea.

"Melvin!" I shouted.

"You rang?" he asked, shimmering into sight at the foot of
my bed.

"I just figured out my third wish." I took a breath. "I want
you to turn Butch Carrigan blue."

15

He looked at me for a moment. Then his eyes went wide. "Vincent," he said, "I like the way you think. I'll be back in a flash."

When he returned he was grinning like a cat.

"You've still got one wish left, kiddo," he said with a chuckle. "Butch Carrigan was already blue as a summer sky when I got there."

If I caused you any trouble with Blueday, I'm sorry. But not much. Because things are never going to be the same now that it happened. Never.

And my third wish?

I've decided to save it for when I really need it—maybe when I meet the girl of my dreams.

Or Prince Charming.

Whichever.

BRUCE COVILLE

I was born in Syracuse, New York, and grew up around the corner from my grandparents' dairy farm, three miles outside a small town called Phoenix. The first time I thought I would like to be a writer was in sixth grade, when our teacher gave us an extended period of time to write a long story. I loved what I wrote, and started planning my first book. (Alas, I never did get around to writing that one.)

Though I am known primarily for middle-grade books such as *Jeremy Thatcher, Dragon Hatcher*, and (most especially) *My Teacher Is an Alien*, I have done work for older audiences as well, including four "teen terror" novels in the early 1980s. I even used to edit a magazine for retired people!

While "Am I Blue?" is not autobiographical (I was never lucky enough to have a fairy godfather), it does reflect many of the confusions I have had in my own life, not only as a teenager but as an adult.

My greatest concern while writing the story was the character of Melvin, primarily because he can be read as an easy stereotype of a certain kind of gay man. But stereotypes often have a solid base in reality, and while Melvin *is* a type, he is also as accurate a portrayal as I could offer of some of the funniest and most gallant men I have ever met—including my dear friend Pete Blair, who died of AIDS some time ago.

WE MIGHT AS WELL ALL BE STRANGERS

▽

by M. E. Kerr

I t was *Christmas*," said my grandmother, "and I went from the boarding school in Switzerland with my roommate, to her home in Germany.

"She was afraid it would not be grand enough for me there . . . that because my family lived in New York, it would seem too modest, and she kept saying, 'We live very simply,' and she kept saying, 'Except for my uncle Karl, who pays my tuition, we are not that rich.'

"I told her no, no, this is thrilling to me, and I meant it. Everywhere there was Christmas: wreaths of *Tannenbaum* hung, the Christmas markets were still open in the little towns we passed through. Every house had its *Christbaum*—a tall evergreen with a star on top.

"I was not then a religious Jew. I was a child from a family that did not believe in religion . . . and what I felt was envy, and joy at the activity: the Christmas-card landscape, snow falling, smoke rising from chimneys, and villagers rushing through the streets with gift-wrapped packages, and the music of Christmas.

21

"Then we saw the signs outside her village.

"*Juden unerwünscht.* (Jews not welcome.)

"And other, smaller signs, saying things in German like kinky hair and hooked noses not wanted here, and worse, some so vile I can't say them to you.

"'These have nothing to do with us,' Inge said. 'These are just political, to do with this new chancellor, Hitler. Pay no attention, Ruth.'

"I did not really even think of myself as a Jew, and while I was shocked, I did not take it personally since I was from America. We even had our own Christmas tree when I was a tiny child. . . . Now I was *your* age, Alison. Sixteen.

"Her parents rushed out to greet us, and welcome us. Inside there was candlelight and mistletoe and wonderful smells of food cooking, and we were hungry after the long trip. The house was filled with the family, the little children dressed up, everyone dressed up and joyous.

"We sat around a huge table, and wine was served to the adults, and Inge's mother said we girls could have half a glass ourselves. We felt grown-up. We sipped the wine and Christmas carols played over the radio, but there was so much talk, it was like a thin sound of the season with in front of us the tablecloth, best china, crystal glasses! I thought, What does she mean she lives modestly? There were servants . . . and it looked like a little house from the outside only. Inside it was big and lively, with presents under the tree we would open later. I was so impressed and delighted to be included.

"Then a maid appeared and in a sharp voice said, 'Frau Kantor? There is something I must say.'

"Inge's mother looked annoyed. 'What *is* it?'

"Then this thin woman in her crisp white uniform with the black apron said, 'I cannot serve the food. I do not hand food to a man, woman, or child'—her eyes on me suddenly—'of Jewish blood ever again.'"

My grandmother paused and shook her head.

I said, "What happened then?"

"Then," my grandmother said, "we carried our plates into the kitchen and served ourselves. . . . All except for Inge's uncle Karl, who left because he had not known until that moment that I was Inge's *Jewish* friend from her school."

"I never heard that you were there when all of that was going on, Grandma."

"It was my one and only time in Germany," she said. "So you don't have to tell me about what it feels like to be an outsider. You don't have to tell me about prejudice. But Alison, I thank you for telling me about yourself. I'm proud that you told me first."

A week later, my mother said, "Why do you have to *announce* it, Alison?"

"Is that all you're going to say?"

"No, that's first. First I'm going to say there was no need to announce it. You think I don't know what's going on with you and Laura? I don't need eyes in the back of my head to figure that out."

"But it makes you uncomfortable to *hear* it from me, is that it?"

"I can't do anything about it, can I? I see it every time you bring her here. I would like to believe it's a stage you're going

23

through, but from what I've read and heard, it isn't."

"No. It isn't."

"I can kiss grandchildren good-bye, I guess, if you persist with this choice."

"Mom, it's not a choice. Was it a choice when you fell in love with Dad?"

"Most definitely. I chose him!"

"What I mean is—you didn't choose him over a woman."

"I would never choose a woman, Alison! Never! Life is family. Or I *used* to think it was. Before *this*!"

"What I mean is—there were only males you were attracted to."

"Absolutely! Where you got this—it wasn't from *me*."

"So what if the world was different, and men loved men and women loved women, but you were still *you*? What would you do?"

My mother shrugged. "Find another world, I guess."

"So that's what *I* did. I found another world."

"Good! Fine! You have your world and I have mine. Mine happens to be the *real* world, but never mind. You always went your own way."

Then she sighed and said, "I'm only glad your father's not alive to hear his favorite daughter tell him she's *gay*."

"I was his *only* daughter, Mother."

"All the more reason. . . . We dreamed of the day you'd bring our grandchildren to us."

"That's still an option. I may bring a grandchild to you one day."

"Don't."

"Don't?"

"Not if it's one of those test-tube/artificial-insemination children. I'm talking about a real child, a child of our blood, with a mother *and* a father. I don't care to have one of those kids I see on Donahue who was made with a turkey baster or some other damn thing! Alison, what you've gotten yourself involved in is not just a matter of me saying Oh, so you're *gay*, fine, and then life goes on. What you've gotten yourself involved in is *serious!*"

"That's why I'm telling you about it."

"That's not why you're telling me about it!"

"Why am I telling you about it?"

"You want me to say it's okay with me. You gays want the whole world to say it's okay to be gay!"

"And it isn't."

"No, it is *not!* Okay? I've said how I feel! You are what you are, okay, but it is not okay with me what you are!"

"So where do we go from here?"

"I'll tell you where not to go! Don't go to the neighbors, and don't go to my friends, and don't go to your grandmother!"

"What do you think Grandmother would say?"

"When she stopped weeping?"

"You think she'd weep?"

"Alison," my mother said, "it would *kill* your grandmother!"

"You think Grandma wouldn't understand?"

"I *know* Grandmother wouldn't understand! What is to

25

understand? She has this grandchild who'll never bring her great-grandchildren."

"I might bring her some straight from the Donahue show."

"Very funny. *Very* funny," my mother said. Then she said, "Alison, this coming-out thing isn't working. You came out to me, all right, I'm your mother and maybe you had to come out to me. But where your grandmother's concerned: Keep quiet."

"You think she'd want that?"

"I think she doesn't even *dream* such a thing could come up! She's had enough *tsuris* in life. Back in the old country there were relatives lost in the Holocaust! Isn't that enough for one woman to suffer in a lifetime?"

"Maybe that would make her more sympathetic."

"Don't compare gays with Jews—there's no comparison."

"I'm both. There's prejudice against both. And I didn't choose to be either."

"If you want to kill an old woman before her time, tell her."

"I think you have Grandmother all wrong."

"If I have Grandmother all wrong," said my mother, "then I don't know her and you don't know me, and we might as well all be strangers."

"To be continued," I wrote in my diary that night.

My grandmother knew . . . my mother knew . . . one day my mother would know that my grandmother knew.

All coming-out stories are a continuing process.

Strangers take a long time to become acquainted, particularly when they are from the same family.

M. E. KERR

"We Might As Well All Be Strangers" was inspired by a story a Jewish psychoanalyst once told me about a visit in Germany when she was a teenager, just after Hitler had come to power.

I told a friend of mine about it, after she had "come out" to her old Jewish grandmother despite her mother's warning that the old lady couldn't take it.

To my friend's amazement, her grandmother was the only sympathetic member of the family. She told her grandchild that she had seen more than enough of prejudice in her lifetime, and asked to meet "your girlfriend."

The two incidents were the basis for my short story.

Night Kites, written in 1983, was the first young adult book to deal with AIDS. It is the story of a young man who returns to his small town very ill. Now he must tell his adoring younger brother, and family, that he is gay and dying.

My most recent award was the American Library Association's Margaret A. Edwards Award (1993) honoring an author's lifetime achievement—specifically for *Dinky Hocker Shoots Smack!*, *Gentlehands*, *Me Me Me Me Me: Not a Novel*, and *Night Kites*.

Linger is my latest book, a novel about the Gulf War.

WINNIE AND TOMMY

by *Francesca Lia Block*

*T*he air smelled like muffins baking and about to burn, and the man's voice on the radio sang sweet and hoarse. Tommy drove his yellow Karmann Ghia over the bridge into a city that seemed made of honey and charcoal.

Winnie thought that she was probably the happiest she had ever been in all her seventeen years. She never had to go back to high school. Michael Stipe was singing "This One Goes Out to the One I Love." She was in love with the hottest skateboarding guy in Santa Cruz, and they were going to spend a whole weekend in San Francisco.

There was nobody like Tommy. He could fly on his skateboard. He had heavy-lidded blue eyes and soft lips that made him look like the angels in Renaissance paintings, and he could draw Renaissance angels, cars, portraits, and almost anything else. He wanted to go to Italy to study art. He was tan and wiry and he knew the names of flowers; he could dance. Animals always came

31

over to him first. He wore the best chunky-puppy shoes instead of the narrow-weasel shoes that some guys wore.

Winnie and Tommy had been going out for a year. They had met at a party at the end of last summer. The air had smelled like beer and trees and had the beginning creep of chill that told everyone school was going to be starting soon. Winnie was drunk on keg beer; she was wearing a tiny black dress and combat boots. She saw Tommy and started dancing by herself nearby, whirring like a Frisbee. When she was dancing, Winnie felt the safest, as if no one could hurt her. Tommy danced too. He could do things like falling into splits and spinning on his back. He and Winnie jammed and slammed, hiphopping until it was light. Then they went to the beach and she sat huddled in a woven Mexican blanket while he surfed. They ate whole-grain pancakes in a natural foods place, and Tommy laughed because Winnie could eat as much as he could even though she was even tinier than he was. Winnie didn't want the time with Tommy to end. When she had to go back to her house, she felt the stone of loneliness sinking down through her body again. She had forgotten about it since she and Tommy had started dancing.

During the whole school year Winnie and Tommy were always escaping together to skateboard, play pinball on the pier, eat poppy-seed cake, look at art books, just drive and drive listening to music. After a while they told each other what they were trying to get away from.

Winnie said, "Our house is like a tomb. It's like my mom died when he did."

Winnie's dad was killed when she was twelve. He had been an architect and built their house by the sea. He had also built Winnie huge, turreted sand castles and called her his merbaby and given her shells and showed her how if you put them in water all their original brilliant color came back. When she cried, he let her listen to his magical conch, told her to take three deep breaths, and promised she would fall into a sleep of beautiful deep-sea dreams. It always worked.

Now there was just her and her mom and whatever new boyfriend her mom brought home that night.

Tommy said, "Your dad probably is still around you in a way. I believe in that stuff. Maybe he's like your guardian angel."

Winnie knew what he meant. Once she was driving home from a party drunk and her mom's car spun out and careened across the street but she wasn't hurt at all and the station wagon was only scratched. That was one time she was sure her dad had been around. She never got behind a wheel drunk again after that.

She wished someone had been her dad's guardian angel the night his motorcycle crashed.

"At least you had a father who really loved you," Tommy said.

"Tell me about your dad."

"He's a bastard."

Winnie ran her fingertip along the lines ridging Tommy's forehead.

"He'd back up the car to the edge of a cliff with me in the

backseat. I was like three. He'd just crack up when I screamed."

"Oh God."

"And he did things like he told me he and I were going to Europe. He packed my bags and everything. I think I was five. All I really wanted in the world was to go to Europe and see the paintings like in the books. He dressed me up and we went to the airport, right to the gate. And then he starts laughing and saying it was just a joke."

"That's sick. What did your mom do?"

"She didn't know about it. I didn't tell her."

"Why?"

"I don't know. I didn't want to upset her. He beat me up too. He broke my arm once. I told my mom I fell down skateboarding. After that I wasn't afraid to do anything on my board."

"Tommy." She saw a flash-image of her dad on his bike, eyes hidden under dark glasses, square jaw, hands gripping the bars. She stopped the picture there.

"And then he left. Thank God. I think the reason I can never stay still is because of him. I read that guys who don't have strong father influences feel like they're spinning all the time."

"I wish I could be your dad," Winnie whispered into Tommy's hair.

"We can be each other's dads."

They were also each other's moms, each making sure that the other had eaten, was dressed warmly enough. Once, while Tommy was teaching Winnie to do a special skateboard jump, he said to her, "You're the son I never had."

She loved that. It was better than if he had said "I love you."

They won Cutest Couple in the school yearbook. They went to the prom in matching baggy black tuxedos. Tommy gave Winnie a corsage of orchids that was almost the size of a centerpiece and must have cost him a week's pay from the skate shop where he worked. He said, "Let's drive to San Francisco the day school gets out."

The first place they went in the city was a tiny Japanese restaurant without a name. A line of people drank beers out of paper bags while they stood outside on Church Street waiting to get in. Tommy asked two handsome men in very soft-looking sweaters if they would purchase some beer for him and Winnie. He had a fake ID, but sometimes it didn't work. The men smiled and one of them took Tommy's money, went to the liquor store on the corner, and bought two huge Sapporos. He handed the paper bags to Tommy. The beers were pearl-dripping with cold and the caps had been opened but half stuck back on. The man gave Tommy his change.

"I think these big ones cost more than that," Tommy said.

"It's okay," said the man, looking into Tommy's eyes.

"Thanks."

Winnie scraped her finger on the edge of the bottle cap as she pulled it off. She shivered as the cold, dark beer poured out of the glass into her mouth. She felt her whole body soften.

The restaurant was so crowded and small, you could hardly walk inside. There was a mural of shy Japanese women peeking out from behind their fans and under their parasols. Some of them were holding babies. The tea smelled sweet, like brown rice. Winnie and Tommy ordered hot miso soup, spinach with sesame sauce, and monster-size California rolls—seaweed cornocopias of fish and thinly sliced, flowery vegetables.

After dinner they walked along Market Street for a while. There were packs of men everywhere. They reminded Winnie of the view of the city from the bridge—beautiful, self-contained, remote. She tried to imitate Tommy's loping boy walk so that she could fit in better.

"Let's go in here," Tommy said.

It was a leather store. There were all kinds of black-leather clothes—tight pants with laces, chaps, halters, studded zippered motorcycle jackets. Winnie tried on black-leather shorts but her zipper got stuck. Tommy had to come into the dressing room to help her.

"Close your eyes, though," she teased.

"How can I do it if my eyes are closed?"

They were both laughing so hard, they thought the slim man with the pierced eyebrow would throw them out. Instead he grinned at Tommy and said, "Why don't you take a look downstairs."

The basement chamber was full of spiked things, rubber things, leather things that Winnie had never seen or even heard of before. Tommy teased her, but then he took her hand as they went back upstairs and bought her a black-leather rose, which he pinned to her jacket.

They drove to the Haight. The street was lined with stores

selling used Levi's, leopard coats, platform shoes, engineer boots, CDs, cappuccino. All the telephone poles and street-lights were plastered with flyers for bands. Kids were hanging out everywhere. Winnie and Tommy gave change to a skinny, big-eyed girl who looked like a kitten. Winnie wished that she and Tommy could have a big house someday and fill it up with street kids and cook meals for them, and that there would be enough love to go around without anyone feeling left out.

Tommy suggested coffee and sugar. They sat in a cafe getting wired on caffeine and poppy-seed cake. Someone had told them that if you ate poppy seeds, your blood would test positive for drugs. They liked to pretend the cake made them high.

When they walked out onto the street, they heard music. Winnie thought it sounded like Gypsies. They stopped to listen. A musician was playing a violin, moving as if completely possessed. The violinist had *cafe au lait* skin, long dark curls, a beautiful face, and an androgynous body that swayed in a puffed-sleeved midriff shirt, tight shorts, and high pirate boots.

"The most beautiful people are the ones that don't look like one race or even one sex," Tommy said.

Winnie thought about this. She knew that with her short brown hair, square jaw, and straight-up-and-down body, with her baggy jeans and big shoes, she looked a little like a boy. She thought that Tommy's eyes and lips made him look prettier than she did sometimes. Once she had put mascara on him for fun and been almost shocked by his beauty.

Winnie pulled his arm. She looked at his face. His eyes

seemed far away as if watching a movie, different from the one she saw.

They walked down the street while the Gypsy violinist, who was not black or white, man or woman, kept playing, the music clicking its heels and snapping its fingers after them.

Winnie wanted to go straight to the hotel, but then they passed a tiny bar and heard blues coming from inside and they both knew they had to dance. The bar smelled of barbecue and beer. They got in with their fake ID's and danced in a crowd of people in front of the little stage. As she pressed against Tommy, Winnie thought their two bodies would melt down and merge into one.

She thought about this the whole way to the Red Vic.

The Red Vic was just that—an old Victorian building painted bright red. There was a movie theater downstairs and a hotel above it. The hotel rooms had special themes—the Rainbow Room, the Rose Garden Room, the Peacock Suite. Winnie and Tommy had the Flower Child Room. There were big psychedelic blossoms everywhere.

The windows of the room looked right out on the still-busy night street where people spare-changed and cars honked, but Winnie felt like she was in another world—a world of yellow daisies and purple peace signs and love-ins, Jimi Hendrix and Janis Joplin.

Winnie went to take a bath. When she got back into the room, smelling of vanilla-almond oil and wearing her silk men's pajamas, Tommy was lying on the bed in his clothes, asleep. She kissed his cheek but he didn't stir. She took off his boots and pulled the covers over him.

"Tommy," she whispered.

He didn't move. Winnie put her arms around him. He was always so warm, like a puppy. His light body got so heavy when he slept. She nestled against him in the Flower Child Room.

As soon as they woke up the next morning, Tommy said, "I have to get some caffeine in me."

He kissed Winnie gently with his soft, full, Italian Renaissance angel lips and got up to bathe.

Winnie and Tommy ate croissants and drank cappuccinos in the Victorian-style parlor full of overstuffed furniture. The croissants tasted too rich for Winnie and the coffee too strong. She felt queasy and still sleepy. Her head pounded.

"Let's get some sun," Tommy said. He was jittery, his knees jumping under the table.

Winnie and Tommy walked along the Panhandle to the park that rolled like a river of grass, trees, hedges, and flowers on its way to the sea. Everything was as green as parks on a map. The rose garden was Tommy's favorite. His mother had taught him all the names of the roses, and Winnie quizzed him as they walked the paths in a haze of fragrance.

Snowfire. Sterling Silver. Smoky. Seashell. Evening Star. Sunfire. Angel Face.

They sat on a stone bench and Tommy read out loud to Winnie from *Franny and Zooey*.

Winnie wanted to say, "I love you." She could taste the

words like frosting on her lips, smell them like the white roses Tommy knew by name.

When they got to Chinatown, the shops were just closing. In the window of the butcher shop dead ducks spread and dangled; there was a pig with cherries for eyes. Fish flickered on the sidewalk in plastic bags. The bakery was full of plump pork buns splitting with filling, sticky wedges of rice pastry, glossy, wet, white noodles, flabby on thin paper and sprinkled with what looked like red and green confetti. People hurried out carrying pink boxes that were already staining with grease. Wind chimes and lanterns made tinkling sounds as the shop owners carried them in for the night. The china bowls painted with peonies and queued children, the tasseled hair ornaments, sandalwood soaps, and teas in willow jasmine boxes were all swept inside. Everything was lush and lacquered, bloodied and slick with grease, broiled and charred and glazed, basted, steamed, sugared.

In an upstairs Chinese restaurant Winnie and Tommy ordered soup and rice and moo shu vegetable with plum sauce.

They found a smoky bar. It was crowded with guys in low-slung jeans and beer-belly-filled T-shirts playing pool while other guys dressed as women in feathers and sequins watched them. A beautiful black blonde in white satin winked at Tommy. Winnie didn't know where to look first.

"I think that angels are like that," Winnie said, admiring a redhead in a green-sequined G-string.

Tommy said, "I don't think she would consider herself an angel."

"You know what I mean. They are so beautiful. More beautiful than men or women. They're like from another world."

"That's true."

"Why is it that the ideal women's legs only come on men?" Winnie said, admiring some shimmering thighs and calves.

Beautiful men-women. Legs. Lips. Mermaid-green sparkle spangles. Silver platform shoes. After a while it was almost too much. Tommy took Winnie's hand and they started to run.

Winnie was running back to the Flower Child Room, but she felt Tommy running away from the city itself—a glam drag queen with roses in her teeth whose face he did not want to see.

When they jumped on the bed, out of breath in the Flower Child Room, Winnie threw her arms around Tommy and pushed him down on his back. She kissed him. But all of a sudden his body felt cold and rigid. It was like he was someone else; she didn't know him. She tried to stroke his thigh, but he shifted away from her.

"What's wrong?"

He shrugged and sat up. Then he said, "I'm trying so hard." He pounded his fist on the bed. Winnie felt the mattress springs contract as if they were inside her body.

"What do you mean?"

"I like guys. I've always liked guys. I kept waiting for it to stop. Or at least to fall in love with someone the way it is with you, so then I would have something concrete. But it's just

41

this feeling. I can't make it stop."

Winnie stared at him, his face hidden in his hands. She remembered when she saw her mother weeping, crawling on the floor, calling Winnie's father's name. The feeling of being alone started then. It stopped five years later, the first time she danced with Tommy.

"How can you tell me this?" Winnie screamed. Her own voice scared her. "I'm your girlfriend."

"If I can't tell you, who am I supposed to tell? My mother? The guys I skate with? You're the only person I can tell. What—I should call my father or something?"

Tommy stood up. He looked like a little boy in his three-waist-sizes-too-big baggy jeans and backward baseball cap. "Okay, fine. I won't talk about it with you. I should have known you'd act like this," he said. He walked to the door.

"Where are you going?"

"I have to get out of here."

She wanted to run to him and hold him and tell him it would be all right as if he were her child, but he wasn't. They were both just children. There was nothing she could say.

Winnie went to the window and waited. She saw Tommy walking down Haight Street looking tiny and young. She wanted to shout for him to come back, but she didn't.

All night she sat huddled in the Flower Child bed. She tried not to move. It was like if she moved, her heart would some-how detach and slip out of place, floating lost in the cavern of her body, deflating like a punctured stray balloon. She held up a mirror and looked at her face. She really did look like a boy—a puffy-faced boy now. She wondered if Tommy had pretended she was a boy when he kissed her. She wondered if her small breasts made him sick. She hated herself. She wanted her dad.

But Tommy is right, she heard her dad say. Who else can he tell except you? You're his best friend. Maybe you're his only friend. Tommy loves you.

Who else will be able to dance like that? Winnie asked her dad. Who else will give me an orchid centerpiece to wear as a corsage? Who will know exactly which shoes we should both get? Who else will draw like that and ride a skateboard like an angel and read out loud to me?

No one, her dad said. Just Tommy.

Well . . .

You'll still have Tommy. You'll find someone else to be your boyfriend. Lots of boys will love you, Merbaby.

That's almost like saying I'll find another dad.

It might feel that way. Maybe you will find someone else to be like your dad. But that doesn't mean you don't have me.

Winnie lay down in the Flower Child bed. She pretended she was on a beach covered with psychedelic daisies, listening to the song of a magical conch shell. She took three deep breaths and fell asleep.

Some time after, so late it was early, Winnie heard the door and opened her eyes. She saw Tommy come into the dark room. He stood in the corner.

"What happened?" Winnie whispered.

"I went to a bar and danced with some guys."

"Was it okay?"

"Yes. But I worried about you."

Winnie turned to him. The pillows were still damp with her tears.

"I don't want you to leave like my dad did."

"I'll never leave you," said Tommy. "It will just be a different thing."

He moved toward her. It must be the light from the window, she thought, because he was radiant like the angels in his favorite paintings. Maybe it was just because something inside him had opened up.

"Can I sleep next to you?" he whispered. He sounded so tired.

Winnie felt the sheets stir as his warm body climbed into the bed. She smelled cigarette smoke and felt the rough fabric of Levi's brush against her bare legs.

Then Winnie and Tommy hugged, wrapped in each other's arms like little children, until they fell asleep.

FRANCESCA LIA BLOCK

I had the idea for "Winnie and Tommy" over ten years ago but have recently rewritten it for *Am I Blue?* I am happy to be included in this important anthology.

While studying English literature at University of California at Berkeley, I began writing my first novel, *Weetzie Bat*. It has subsequently been chosen as an ALA Best Book for Young Adults and an ALA *Booklist* Young Adult Editors' Choice, and a Recommended Book for Reluctant Young Adult Readers. The sequel to *Weetzie Bat*, *Witch Baby*, is a *School Library Journal* Best Book and an ALA Recommended Book for Reluctant Young Adult Readers. *Cherokee Bat and the Goat Guys*, the third book in this series, is a *New York Times* Notable Book, one of *Publishers Weekly*'s 50 Best Books of 1992, an ALA Best Book for Young Adults, and an ALA Recommended Book for Reluctant Young Adult Readers. My adult novel *Ecstasia* has been published, and a second adult novel is forthcoming. I have also recently completed a fourth book in the "Weetzie" series, called *Missing Angel Juan*.

I have also written for *The New York Times*, the *Los Angeles Times*, and *Spin* magazine. Currently I live in California.

SLIPPING AWAY

by Jacqueline Woodson

My mother stands in our summerhouse kitchen cutting ripe cantaloupe into wedges. Sitting by the window, I go back and forth between watching the reflection of her flawless movements and imagining new colors for the weathered gray chairs we have just put out for the season. I am waiting for Maria, so Mama and I say nothing to each other, and the kitchen is quiet save for the sound of metal meeting wood. My mother is tanned, and her skin looks strange against the rush of gray-and-blond hair above her ears. Her linen pants are stained and wrinkled, stopping short above her pale ankles. The moccasins she wears are stretched out and turned over at the heels. She has thrown my father's T-shirt on over a bikini top, and as I watch her reed-thin body jerk with the rhythm of cutting, I wonder what my own body will be like at thirty-eight.

49

"Sometimes," I say into the window, "I think I will keep on growing and never stop! . . ."

My mother turns and frowns at me, then laughs, shaking her head.

I watch her reflection in the pane.

"Dramatics, Jacina," she says, turning back to the melon. "Jacina, the drama queen."

But at twelve I am already five feet seven inches tall, just four inches shorter than my mother. And although she swears I will grow into my height, my breasts are the size of half-eaten gumdrops and my legs are skinny and long.

My mother slices the rind from the last of the melon in one stroke and transfers it from the chopping board into a glass bowl that she sets on the table.

"Going to be a hot summer here," she says, pressing her chin against the top of my head for a moment as she stares out the window. Then, too quickly, she pulls away and goes to rinse her hands at the sink.

"Mama," I say, not knowing what I'll say next but feeling a cold spot where her chin rested and wanting that spot to be warm again.

"Yes?"

"Nothing."

"What, Jacina?"

"Just nothing."

"It'll come back to you," she says mysteriously. She is smiling when I look at her. I stare into her blue eyes for a moment but don't smile back.

My mother is the one closest to me in the world. Then there is my father. It has always been this way—the three of us together alone. In New Rochelle, where we live most of the year, there are a few girls I spend some time with, but we aren't close. Sometimes, watching those girls walking from school, hand in hand, I long for a friend I can be close to, a friend I can walk that way with and share all the things I am thinking. But Mama says it is because I am too quiet and far away from the rest of the world. She says people are afraid of silence. In the summer there is Maria. She is the other person I am closest to, and sometimes, in the winter, I long to call her up and say, "Come here and live with me, in this cold place." But we are summer friends. There is a rule, it seems, that summer friends don't get together in the wintertime. Now, sitting here waiting for her, I realize I have never seen Maria in a winter coat, and for some reason this makes me sadder than anything else in the world.

In the distance a car door slams. I listen. A few moments pass before there is a tap at the living-room window.

"She's here, Mama! She's here!" I scream, jumping off the white vinyl bar stool.

I slam into Maria in the living room. We laugh for no reason at all as she throws her bags on the couch and gives me a shove. I shove her back and we laugh again. She is almost as tall as I am now.

"Hi," I say, catching my breath. Maria is wearing one of the white beach dresses we bought together last August, but hers is too small across the chest where mine still fits fine. Her

51

hair is out and tangled, falling down past her back in a mass of black waves. She pushes it out of her face as she laughs. We stare at each other for an awkward moment. Not knowing what else to do, I reach out to hug her—hard and fast and clumsily. Her arms reach to hug me back, but I have already broken the embrace so they are in midair for a second before dropping back at her sides. We laugh again.

"When'd you get here? Just now?" I ask, motioning her into the kitchen, unsure of the reason for my embarrassment.

"I haven't even gone to my house yet!" Maria says.

My mother has set out peaches beside the cantaloupe and is working on a pan of scrambled eggs and cheese. She kisses Maria's forehead. Maria puts her arm around my mother's waist.

"You look good, Maggie," she says, and even my mother looks a little surprised. "Those pants do a lot for your figure," Maria continues.

"Figure?!" I explode, laughing out loud. They glance at me, and I sink back onto the stool, feeling dumb and young. It would be nice, now, to shrivel into the stool, then disappear. Figure. I wonder if I will ever have one, a nice one, like Mama's and the one Maria is getting. I stare at Maria's hand on my mother's waist until it blurs. Mama says this is natural, to get sad about the silliest things. Hormones. But I know it is more than that. These days, more than ever, I feel as though I am slipping away, floating off, like a cloud or a lost balloon.

"My mother must have gained twenty pounds over the winter," Maria is saying disgustedly. "You have to see her. No . . .

no you don't. You don't have to see her."

"Your mom's pretty," I say, really meaning it. "So what if she gained weight?"

Maria looks at "Maggie" like they're in on a secret, but my mother doesn't return the look, and I am relieved. Instead, she moves the pan to the counter and stares down at the eggs. Maria comes over and sits across from me, smoothing her dress against her lap. She bites off the end of a piece of melon and chews slowly.

"Manhattan was crazy this winter," she says. "There're a lot of people there."

I say nothing and stare at her. All along I have been thinking it is her voice that has done a whole lot of changing. But now I realize it is the way she is talking. Her accent is gone.

"It seems like everybody is moving to the Upper East Side. All these new kids live in our building."

Maria's father is a super on Fifty-fifth and Sutton. The one time I visited her in the spring, the old ladies in the building came outside to give us stale spearmints and pinch our cheeks. They asked if I was visiting from Puerto Rico, and when I told them I wasn't Puerto Rican, that my mother was white and my daddy black, they frowned and reminded Maria to tell her father about their clogged drains and flooding toilets.

"You sound different, Maria."

"My mother keeps saying that, but I always sounded like this."

"No you didn't. You had an accent before."

"I never had an accent," Maria says, getting angry. But the

"t" at the end of "accent" is silent, and I smile. Maria changes the subject.

"Your family is always the first one out, Jacina. You're lucky."

"That's because my father wants to get rid of us as soon as possible so he can do whatever it is he does when we're gone for two months."

I feel a sharp tap on my head and turn to see my mother standing with the handle of a wooden spoon suspended above me.

"Enough, smart mouth," Mama says. She starts to kiss the place on my head, but I duck. Mama shakes her head and turns back to the eggs. I check my hair with my hand and come away with a tiny piece of cheese.

"Don't you miss him, Maggie?" Maria asks.

My mother lets out a small laugh. "I think Nicholas and I have been married long enough to live without each other for a month or two."

"When I get married, me and my husband are going to do everything together. Everything!" Maria pounds the table.

"You can't do new things with a tired old husband following you everywhere, right, Mama?"

Mama laughs again.

"You can't meet new people. There're a lot here this summer. I kept seeing all these cars."

"I know," Maria says, wrinkling her nose. "Mostly lesbos. I saw a whole carful on my way here."

"This is a nice community," my mother warns. "Don't

worry about the lesbians. I'm sure they're not losing any sleep over you two." She says this in that way adults have of making it seem like they're teaching you a lesson rather than scolding you.

"Have you ever heard of Martha's Vineyard?" Maria asks.

I shake my head and turn to my mother.

"Mama, have you?"

My mother nods. "Nick and I thought of buying a house there before we bought this one. We changed our minds."

"Why?" Maria noses.

"It's not a friendly place."

I look at Maria and shrug.

"Orient Point," she continues, "is more tolerant. That's why we chose it. Anyone can live here and not feel like a pariah."

"Oh," Maria says politely, and I know she doesn't under-stand what my mother means.

After Maria takes her things home, we walk to the beach, mostly in silence but occasionally belting out a song at the top of our lungs. Maria has a nice voice but I sing off-key.

The beach is chilly and almost empty when we finally get there. Climbing up onto a rock, Maria and I take a look around. Two women stroll by holding hands, and I wave. They wave back and keep walking. About a hundred yards away, a group of women has started a picnic. The edges of their blanket blow up and over everything. Finally, each takes a place at one of the four corners and stretches to get at the food. Maria and I laugh and sit down. Cold air blows off the water, and I shiver, wishing I had been smart like Maria and worn a sweater.

We talk about nothing for a while, then fall silent for a long time.

"Jacina," Maria says finally.

"Huh?"

"You ever want to go someplace else?"

"Like where?"

"Like somewhere where there are boys and not just lesbos everywhere."

"Not really," I say, because I know that all I want this summer is to be able to go anywhere I want with my mother and not be stared at; not be asked whether I am black or white. And to watch the women up close and see if they are really as my mother says, just like any other couples.

"I do," Maria says.

"There's not only lesbos here. Your dad's here a lot and all those people in town are straight and . . . I don't know. This is where we live in the summer. I like it here. I like it a lot."

Maria doesn't like my answer. I can tell by the way she wrinkles her nose. She busies herself with picking at the rock.

"Why do you think they bring us someplace that has so many anyway?"

"You know good and well why, Maria. Because the people are nice. Everybody's been here since like forever. And your father said so himself, remember? He said he's not going to let the dites chase him out of here."

"Dykes."

"Whatever." I start picking at the rock myself. Who cares?

"I don't know. It just seems dumb. It seems like they want us to grow up and be like that or something."

"Like what?"

"Like those women, stupid."

"The dites?"

Maria looks annoyed. "Yeah, the dykes."

"Are you kidding, Maria? As much as your father bugs us about them? As much as he yells at us to stop hanging out so much with each other and get some boyfriends? Your daddy would rather you be dead or a nun or something!"

"What about your mother? You think she wants you to be one? She's always taking up for them."

I look at Maria for a long time. She stares back at me and I'm the first to drop my gaze. A fear like nothing else I've ever felt before creeps slowly up my spine. Maria. My summer friend. Every summer for as long as anybody could remember. *Remember, Maria,* I want to scream, *how we said we'd grow old together? Just you and me and forever and ever, amen? Please remember it all, Maria. All the promises.* But I am silent again, the silent girl I am all winter, and I feel Maria slipping backward, away from me. Sitting right there but slipping away. And there is no way to catch her. No way to hold on.

"She takes up for them because she says they have a right. You heard her," I say to the water. "She takes up for them because she married my father."

"What does marrying your father have to do with anything?"

This time it's my turn to get annoyed. "My father's black,

remember?" I roll my eyes at her and turn back to the water. Small waves silently approach our rock.

"Oh," Maria says.

"My mother wouldn't care," I say, softly because I am thinking it for the first time. "If I grew up to be a dite, my mother wouldn't care. She would love me the way she does now."

Maybe Maria moves an inch away from me. Maybe I just imagine it.

"Would you?"

Maria folds her arms across her chest and stares out over the water. "Would I what?" she nearly whispers.

"Would you love me? Even though?"

There is a silence between us that is cold and wet as fog. I want to ask again but know she has heard me. When I reach to touch her arm, Maria pulls away. She looks over at the picnickers. They have finished eating now and are cuddled up into two couples. Dark wine bottles and cracker boxes rest beside the blanket.

"I don't know," Maria says. She stares at the couples for a long time. Then, saying nothing, she climbs down from the rock and heads up the beach away from them. I wait for her to come back. Rain clouds blow in off the water and stagger above our rock. In the mist, my hair kinks up around the edges like Daddy's and blows into my eyes, my ears, my mouth. I pull my knees up to my chin and wrap my arms around them. Sandpipers dart along the shore. I watch them, waiting.

Soon, the picnickers pack up and head down the beach, becoming four dots in the distance.

Mama says everything falls into place somehow and even the craziest things eventually start to make sense. She says we have to be strong and brave and patient. . . .

Two women walk by with a black puppy. They wave but I don't wave back.

I am too busy waiting.

JACQUELINE WOODSON

Whenever I am asked to write about myself, I always get tongue-tied. What is there to say? My friends know who I am. They would say that I laugh easily and love living, that maybe I work a little too much and don't play enough. I don't know. I'd have to agree. What else? I walk like someone unsure of her next step at times and often I am shy around new people. Sometimes I feel that I am too tall, that my hair is weird, that my nose is too big. Sometimes people say I'm pretty and I believe them. I don't like wasting my money on bad movies. I listen to music all the time. I write all the time, and when I'm not writing, I'm thinking about it. My favorite books that I've written are *I Hadn't Meant to Tell You This* and *The Dear One*. I have a book being published that's going to take me on tour, and that makes me nervous. If I couldn't write, I don't think I'd be able to live. Once I heard Dorothy Allison, another writer, say, "Tell your stories," and it was one of the most important things anyone ever said. Every story is valid. I'd love to hear other people's stories. Our lives are all so different: who we are, who we are becoming . . . I wish everyone had the courage to write. I wish there weren't so much hate and fear in the world. I am hoping, through my writing, I can change the way people think about things a little bit, and thus, in some way or another, change a little bit of the world.

THE HONORARY SHEPHERDS

SHEPHERDS

by Gregory Maguire

In memory of James Masso
and Zac Watts

*T*o *satisfy* that particular curiosity first: Yes, this is a story about two boys who sleep together. Eventually. Not genitally, or anyway not at the time of this writing. But focus, liberally as you like, on the picture of it. Two teenage boys on a single-size futon, under a fraying tangerine-colored afghan reeking of mothballs. Two guys. Warm, scared. Unbelieving. Alive. Cautious. Too alert, too new to each other to giggle or wisecrack. They are both beautiful, at least to each other. The casting department of a film company might not agree.

Sex sells everything, even sex you might disapprove of. That's why the image of the boys abed starts this story. It used to be stories could work up to such a development. But in the current day there's no time for the slow buildup. Notice how movie musicals are passé? Now we make do with three-minute music videos. Notice how often the trailers they show at Cineplex 1–12 are more interesting than the ninety-eight-minute feature film you've paid good money to see? In the future there will be no movies, only coming attractions. No symphonies, only advertising jingles. No novels, only short stories. Maybe only postcards. Vignettes.

The camera is about to leave this opening vignette, and not return, so take it all in while you can. The afghan slips off in a manner suspiciously gratifying of our natural voyeurism. The censors of frontal nudity need not be alarmed—both boys are lying on their stomachs. Their naked legs and behinds, the hollows of their backs, are striped honey and charcoal by the bars of strengthening dawn light falling diagonally across them. Deep in blue-purple shadow from the neck up, they turn their heads so they can look at each other's faces at close range. Three inches apart. Two inches. One.

Freeze frame. Check color registration: cobalt-purple shadow, tangerine blanket. Lips are gray-rose.

Cut.

The younger of the two boys is Lee Rosario Kincaid. Lee's family is Puerto Rican, Polish, and Irish. Not to get overly schematic, but he is the thinker of the two. The older, Pete Blake, is the gutted, trembling one. Pete's mom is Chinese and his dad is, was, an American black—from western Africa, Gambia probably, all those troubled generations ago. Between them the boys represent the gene pools of four continents. It's the melting-pot thing carried to absurdity, but it's true. Full-blooded American boys. These things happen.

Lee Rosario Kincaid has wound a school scarf around his

neck and drawn the afghan up to his armpits. His shoulders are white, like the porcelain on old faucet fixtures. He tells Pete Blake about his background:

It's pure U. S. of A. Contrary cultures meet in melting-pot America and fall in love. It's, like, West Side Story II. *That's how I imagine it. The story of my life.*

Start in 1959—my grandparents' generation. Remember Tony and Maria in the movie? After the rumble, after Tony the Polack kills Maria the Spic's brother, she runs to Tony anyway, in true love? But Tony gets shot. Maria catches the falling hero. Love should be stronger than hate. Across their ethnic differences, true love. It's great.

When they showed that movie at Dunster Institute, at an assembly, everyone laughed, except the girls. (Some of the girls did laugh, harder than the guys.) Next day a black kid from a housing project got knifed in the locker room. So much for tolerance.

Here's what happened next, though. As I imagine it. Maria is pregnant from her one ecstatic wedding night with Tony. What do you think "One Hand, One Heart" was all about, anyway? This was pre-AIDS, and people didn't have condoms in their pockets and pocketbooks all the time. They made love. Tony and Maria. I hope it was wonderful, because it was Tony's only time.

Maria's family sends her back to Puerto Rico to have the baby. Rita Moreno has to go too, to chaperone her. She is bored stiff the whole time. Who wants to do hot-tamale dances with big white teeth clicking like castanets for an eight-months-pregnant steamboat? That's not how she cares to spend her time. The baby is born, though: They name her Antonetta. That's my mom, who really is half Polish and half Puerto Rican. And her name is Antonetta. A little bit of Hispanic-Polish bacon. Maria sings "There's a Place for Us" to get the baby to go to sleep at three in the morning.

After a while momma and baby go back to the West Side in New York. They're tearing down the slums to build Lincoln Center. Antonetta grows up hated for being part Polack. She learns to make galumpkes like the best of them, though.

At a bar in Queens in 1975, when she's sixteen, Antonetta meets up with Brendan Kincaid, an illegal immigrant from County Cork, Ireland. A couple of beers too many, and not having learned the family lesson, Antonetta conceives me. Brendan, being Irish Catholic, marries her on the spot. Grandma Maria by 1975 has gotten dumpy and is still trailing around Lincoln Center in that same virginal white dress. (She's had to have her seamstress friends take it out at the sides three times.) She misses Tony still, but she curses her daughter Antonetta for making the same mistake she did.

But surprise, surprise—Antonetta and Brendan are happily married. They get a better deal of it than Maria and Tony did. Nobody shoots Brendan. He turns into a good father, moves the little family to Poughkeepsie, starts his own roofing concern. He's pretty happy.

Until the day—yet to come—he will learn that his only

son, Lee Rosario Kincaid, is gay. Then he might begin to
wish he'd used a condom seventeen years ago.

Pete Blake laughs at this story. The kind of laugh that has a
knowing wince knitted all through it. He's not sure what
parts of this family history are true, but there sits Lee Rosario
Kincaid across from him in his bed, a face as grim as
Churchill's. Lee has the turniplike forehead of the Irish, a
complexion of scalded milk like the Polish, and dark hair, iron
rigid in its curls, like the Puerto Ricans. Lee thinks he is
hideous. He isn't good-looking, it's true, except in love: but
he is striking.

Pete Blake is *gorgeous* but doesn't know it.

He can't tell Lee his story in so dramatic a fashion. It
comes out in sentence fragments, reservations, ellipses,
breathy hesitations. Lee finally pieces it together as such:

Pete Blake's mom is from Boston's Chinatown. His dad is
from Mattapan, a ghetto-grim place to be from and hard to
get out of. Religion never entered into their story, at least not
to hear Pete tell it. They got married. Pete's dad was a professional soldier, not a draftee, and he didn't get killed in
Vietnam but died in a Jeep crash in the Philippines in 1979.
His mom went back to live with her Chinese-speaking family
above—you guessed it—a dim sum restaurant.

Pete is part black, part Chinese.

His mom's family hates him for looking so black.

His dad's family loved him, but that was before. They were

a small family and they died off. An uncle got shot in a gun-fight. A grandma died of grief, or obesity, or both. A cousin got a scholarship to Princeton and left and never came back. Pete would go wandering around the littered sidewalks of Mattapan where his black grandma once lived, missing her. Pete adored his mom, but she had little time for him, chopping ginger and spring onions and studying the pattern in which they fell on the chopping board rather than the pattern of her son's need.

South Boston High was lousy with racial trouble. Pete, taking a clue from his cousin's escape, got the guidance counselor to do some work for a change. Pete Blake applied to Dunster Institute, a fancy private high school in upstate New York. A boarding school. He got in. Full scholarship.

His mom was pissed. His Chinese relatives were relieved and gave him money on the sly to ensure his departure. Pete had never stopped being a mighty shame to them—those sensual negroid lips, that very un-Asian fanny that stuck out like a bumper on a car.

The color. The browned oak-leaf color. Unacceptable. Shaming.

Pete Blake didn't have so much of a problem being gay because he'd hardly had time to realize it yet. It was being neither Chinese nor black that bothered him. He was so twisted up inside about it, too, that he had no idea how tormentingly handsome he was.

He would probably learn, and in the sad—or maybe lucky—irony of it, he would figure it out only after his beauty had begun to fade.

▼

This story has a plot, and here it goes.

Lee and Pete are just meeting each other for the first time. It's a film seminar, senior elective. The class consists of fourteen kids. Some brainy girls who dress in black and never smile. The usual three or four girls who take any course Pete Blake takes, because he smites them so with true lust. A couple of jocks who mistakenly think a film class will be easy sailing and boost their grade-point averages (it won't and it doesn't). Pete, of course, always looking for images of himself to relate to. And Lee, who is a junior but his good grades permit a few allowances, like entry into this class.

The plot is *not* about how Lee and Pete meet and fall in love, or only tangentially so. They're both still a bit in the dark about sex, and while they've heard all about sexual preference liberty, they haven't thought it applied to them. But they do notice each other in the classroom. They also both notice the teacher, a Ms. Cabbage. Sounds as if the name has been changed to protect the innocent or amuse the readers, but it's real: Violet Cabbage. She is mid-forties, thick waisted, sharp as a tack, wears a wig because of chemotherapy treatments, and has a husband named Dennis who has pecs like watermelons and adores her.

Ms. Cabbage starts the class on thinking about myths. Myths are the understructure of culture, she says. Everything we have an opinion about is supported in one of our cultural myths. Nobody knows what she means. She adjusts her wig, about which she makes no pretense. Then she takes it off. It sits in her hand like the pelt of a raccoon. Her baldish head startles, even scares students.

"The myth of beauty," she says, "says that beauty is the outward sign of inner moral goodness. As, weekly, I become less beautiful, I fear the loss of my moral value. What are the myths that teach me this equation? That beauty and goodness are related?"

Lee, who is quick off the mark, shoots his hand up. "Sleeping Beauty."

"She wasn't good," says Violet Cabbage. "She was neutral."

"She wasn't *bad*," says Lee, "which is almost the same thing as being good. In the United States of Amnesia. Where apathy is king."

"Point taken. Don't be a smart-ass. Anyone else?"

Everyone stares and looks stupid. "Christian art," says Ms. Cabbage. "You ever see a homely Madonna? Mary is innocent and pure and so she has to be perfectly made. Ravishing. Naturally, being good, she's not aware of her beauty and so has no sin of pride in her magnificent features."

"Snow White," says Pete, the only black (or golden-brownish) kid there.

"Better than Sleeping Beauty," agrees Ms. Cabbage, "because it's her selfless beauty that inflames her stepmother, the queen."

"Beauty and the Beast," says someone, and Violet Cabbage does a creditable imitation of crackly-voiced Angela Lansbury as Jessica Fletcher, solving the mystery of virtue and appearance. "Tale as old as time . . ." she sings.

She stops. "Tale as old as time," she repeats sternly. "That's myth. Now the modern versions. Move from the beauty of Mary and the female saints, in Western European culture, from the beauty of Venus and the Three Fates, to Guinevere, the beauty of Britannia, the romantic statues of blind Justice governing the courthouses of the land, the film stars of the twenties, and so on. A direct link."

"Guinevere was a hussy," says Lee, bravely, because really he's not supposed to be in this class and shouldn't be rocking the boat so early, but he's afraid of being thought slow because he's a junior, so he's overcompensating. "Gorgeous Natalie Wood as Maria in *West Side Story* probably slept with Tony. Premaritally. Which as Catholics means they'd both go to hell."

"But they suffer for it, don't they," says Ms. Cabbage. "Tony dies and Maria is left all alone. They're redeemed by their suffering, so Maria is still beautiful during the closing credits." She is getting a bit off course, and tacks them back on target. "Ten minutes. Pair off. Discuss the myths that created your sense of yourself. Count off, one-two." They count off. Lee and Pete (oh the cleverness of the beautiful Fates!) are a pair. They don't look at each other, and mumble out of mutual glum shyness.

Here the scene changes gratuitously. Because these days you can't be expected to have an attention span of longer than two pages. No offense intended. It's all a result of too much TV, just as they say.

A flash forward. It's a Saturday. Lee takes the bus from his house in Hyde Park and meets Pete at the school gate. Pete has a video camcorder. They have gotten teamed up for a semester project and want to familiarize themselves with the school's equipment. Dunster Institute, despite its sobriquet as Dumpster Institute, is well endowed in the audio-visual department.

If this story ever gets bought for an AfterSchool TV special, please note: The soundtrack of this montage should be more staccato than legato. No strings. High-hat, cymbals, maybe something mysterious like Andean pipes or polyphonic chanting, but quick. Jumpy. This isn't the bit about puppy love. The boys are devilish.

They are coming to know each other, not by unimpeded observation but by looking at each other through the camera. And by being looked at. Pete walks on the back of a park bench as if it's a balance beam. Lee holds the camera at shoulder height, which exaggerates the bulge of both crotch and bum. Pete does a gymnastic thing and slips. The film keeps rolling as Lee drops the camera, and the film will show only fallen leaves and the underside of a van parked at the curb as Lee puts his hands on Pete for the first time, scared that Pete has hurt himself badly. He hasn't, actually, but Pete lies there not even knowing he's pretending to be winded. Not knowing the reason why: because Lee leaves his hands, lightly but tellingly, on the frayed lapels of Pete's denim jacket.

Remember: no strings.

No strings attached.

Not yet.

Pete grumpily gets up at last and hobbles to reclaim the camcorder. It's Lee's turn in front of the lens. Lee, who is less athletic than Pete, becomes verbal, spouting lines of poetry, doing imitations of the teachers, including Ms. Cabbage, then Bette Midler (being campy without knowing what camp is, or why), then, devastatingly, an imitation of Pete. Lowering his eyelashes in that unconscious denial of beauty that makes Pete the more enticing. Sucking in his gut and moving with a dancer's airy gracefulness. Pete is awed at Lee's ruinous talent at mimicry, and ashamed of how he is seen. Lee, of course, can't feed Pete's beauty back to him, because Lee doesn't have it; so what Pete reads is narcissism and self-love, exactly the opposite of what he feels, and just as ugly, though in a different way, as self-hatred.

"Let's stop," says Pete, still filming.

"Don't stop," says Lee, in a voice still imitating Pete's. "Don't stop, Lee! Film me! Let me reveal to the *world* my immense love for you! I can't help myself! Hee hee hee!" The laughs are in Lee's real voice, not in Pete's copied one, for Pete has set the camera down and he has run to tackle Lee into the rustling blanket of maple leaves. They both yell and squeal and wrestle, and if you must read this as foreshadowing sex despite my instructions, I can't stop you. But Pete is mostly angry, and his punches and jabs really hurt Lee, who is confused and doesn't know what he's done wrong.

What should come next is a dialogue, a painful one. It's several weeks later. November is cupping its cold hands around our boys. Key colors: slate, pumpkin, brown. Aromas: coffee, burning leaves (though illegal, people still do it), the cold dull stink of soil turned over for the planting of spring bulbs. For background music cue in the Adagio of Shostakovich's Second Piano Concerto. Neither Lee nor Pete is especially interested in classical music, but struggling to identify their growing friendship with something outside themselves, they notice a poster announcing a famous pianist coming to Vassar College. They attend, the youngest members of the audience. Lee is beginning to notice how Pete attracts the glances of women and men alike. This makes Lee think, first time, the dynamite question. Am I *attracted* to him? And does that mean . . . ?

Yikes.

The dialogue follows in a Greek diner downtown. The coffee comes in paper cups with a picture of the Acropolis printed in Aegean blue between borders of the Greek key design. Editorial advice about this story, however, suggests fifteen typed pages *max*. So I'll skip the dialogue.

It's the ugly one, the lying one. How many girls they've come on to, and how successfully. Neither Pete nor Lee is given to lying, but fear prompts them. Maybe this conversation isn't very different whether it's between boys or between girls, between straight or gay kids. You can fill in the blanks yourself. If you're lucky, you outgrow this kind of sneakiness. If you're strong, you don't need it.

Well, that's *my* myth anyway: Lying is weak. But I guess there are situational complexities. And an ideal, after all, is something to aim for.

Each one is acutely aware of his own lies, of course. As Pete leans past Lee to pay the cashier on the way out, brushing into Lee's side from hip to shoulder, it's as if their clothes have heat-melted away and they've touched private skin for those twenty inches. Then they each know that the other has been lying, and rather than draw them together this divides them. They pretend a boredom, a nonchalance, as they part. And this pretense gives them both the creeps.

Now, quixotically, the focus of this story changes. You'll see why I started it with naked boys in bed when I tell you it now veers into religion. If I'd started with religion, whoever would have bothered to read this far?

Lee and Pete have fallen in love. But let's leave them their pet names, their explorations, their little alibis, and especially their fears of AIDS. They will get through things okay; they're smart and the school distributes pamphlets, much to the loud chagrin of some parents. They are each other's worlds, for a while. Terrified, they're also inspired. It doesn't escape the notice of Ms. Cabbage, but frankly she has other things on her mind, namely her health, which is deteriorating. Also she's secretly pleased for both of them, but of course if she let it be known, she'd probably be sacked, and she needs her health insurance now more than ever.

The end-of-semester assignment is a big one. They can work independently or in pairs. They are to rewrite a myth and film it.

Naturally Pete and Lee are working on it together. They

meet in Pete's room in the dorm and sit in each other's laps and stroke each other's hair and kiss each other, gently, and jump up from time to time to check the lock on the door, which is always still locked, of course. Eventually they get down to work. At first Lee wants to remake *West Side Story*, showing a very pregnant Maria coming back into the ghetto with an Uzi or something. But Pete correctly points out that *West Side Story* is already the reworking of older myths and stories, and they should get to the root of something.

They are becoming bolder through their love of each other. (In a bookstore Lee has found two postcards of David Hockney's painting *We Two Boys Together Clinging*, and with blushing courage bought them; the postcards mark their places in whatever books they're reading at the moment.) Pete suggests they redo a myth that has rendered the world only in heterosexual images, to create a place for themselves there. "There's a Place for Us," he sings, to tease Lee and to tempt him to say yes.

Of course this is a bold move, but they both know that Ms. Cabbage is dying, and in an unspoken way they want to show her she is helping them change their lives. So maybe they'll be shunned by their classmates or laughed at. So what? They'll deal with that when it comes, they say to each other, through their innocence blissfully unaware of how much it may hurt.

But what myth to rewrite? First they think of stereotypes of gay guys. Chisel-jawed, lean and rich and white and strong, coolly aloof from society, from family, from the past, from attachments of any sort except sex. Both Pete, with his aching and unanswerable need of Chinese and black American families, and Lee, whose dad is going to throw up when he learns Lee is gay, hate this modern myth, this stereotype. "I don't want to be alone," says Pete. "I want to be with you, first" (time out for some distracting nuzzling) "and I want to belong to my families and cultures still. Why should I allow myself to be kicked out?"

Lee feels the same, and only now realizes it. He's proud of the Puerto Rican in his blood, and of the Polish, and the Irish. And what binds them all together, he realizes with a gulp, is the Catholicism. The only thing he is, on all sides, besides American, is Catholic. All his genes have been Catholic for a thousand years or more.

"Can't be Catholic and gay," says Pete, who doesn't actually know. "Pope says so. I think."

"Why should I allow myself to be kicked out?" Lee feeds Pete's words right back to him. "Besides, you can't be kicked out of a *faith*. Faith starts inside your heart and ends up in eternity. All you can be kicked out of is a building, which is the bus stop of faith, sort of, and what's a building?"

And that's how they make their final project, called "The Honorary Shepherds." Since all the fellow students are helping each other, Pete and Lee talk one of the jocks into being Joseph, and one of the girls permanently in a black turtleneck to be Mary. They use a toolshed out by the football field for the stable, and a clamp light hidden in some weeds to be the light of the baby Jesus in the crib. The music is maybe a little too avant-garde a choice: snatches of the Adagio of

79

Shostakovich's Second Piano Concerto. But they've come to think of it as their song. An indulgence.

And what the six-minute video shows is this:

Night sky. Stars. Sheep. (Real sheep—there's a sheep farm about twelve miles out of Poughkeepsie, and since it's been an unseasonably warm fall, the sheep aren't penned in for the night yet. A lucky stroke.) No music. Lee and Pete, in bathrobes and towels just like kindergartners in a pageant, are crouched around a dying campfire. They break a baguette and share it. Nobody speaks in the whole film, since no one knows what Aramaic sounds like and it's already weird enough to have a half-Chinese-half-black shepherd in the hills in the suburbs of Bethlehem.

The camera lingers on the touch of hands, one shepherd to another. It is a warming touch, a touch of friendship. There are other shepherds on the hills, farther away. (Some are the girls in the class, and this is important to Lee and Pete, but it doesn't come out very clearly in the finished project.) From across the fields there are glances and waves as the various shepherds settle down for the night. Lee and Pete sit close, shivering, and then closer, to keep warm, apparently. Pete's arm encircles Lee and Lee's head goes onto Pete's shoulder. (They've discussed renting fake beards but discarded that idea early.) It's not a sex film. It's a film about love.

The music starts. The boys sit up, first apart from each other in fear, then their arms encircling each other, looking all about. Some fancy camera work (Pete read how in a book) having to do with photographing the reflection of light on water, using mirrors. It looks stagey and amateur, but you get the idea. It's like a comet. It's like the end of the world. It's like the beginning of the world.

The boys begin to run. Stumbling and helping each other, wheeling arms, spinning robes showing stretches of leg. In the final version even Pete can't deny that he is stunningly photogenic.

Cut to the inside of the stable.

The camera doesn't linger here, just enough to give you the traditional idea. Traditional and radical too, *radical* meaning root, at the root: This is Christianity at the root, where it all began. The child who would be the Christ, and grow up to preach the gospel of love, is ably portrayed by the 150-watt bulb. No matter what else has happened to Christianity, the story could certainly tolerate this: that among the grizzled, careworn shepherds there might have been two young men, who brought their love for each other with them when they came to adore at the manger. And the proud mother didn't care who loved her wonderful child—how could she care? That's why all children are born: to be loved.

The film ends with a slow, scrutinizing pan over a fifteenth-century nativity scene printed on page 553 of Jansen's *The History of Art*, 1985 edition. A nativity in ochers, attributed to Geertgen tot Sint Jans. The Virgin is, of course, graceful and pure as an egg. The cow is placid. The angels look like Munchkins, disproportionately small to Mary's looming loveliness. Seen through the door of the stable, in the background, is a white blur in the sky, and this is the messenger angel. The distant shepherds are silhouetted, dark forms against the lighted hillside. One is on his knees in fear. Two are standing near each other, shadowy, shoulder to shoulder, close as a couple of lovers. Maybe those are female shepherds farther on, and mixed-race shepherds just on the other side of the hill, and handicapped shepherds in wheelchairs just out of sight. And Buddhist and atheist and vegetarian and every kind of shepherd you can think of.

"Ah," writes Ms. Cabbage, "my only remark is that of course the Holy Birth was always *meant* to be one that would bring people together, not tear them apart. Very fine work, boys. Live out the old myth, pour new life into it. You belong there."

Truth be told, not many of the parents or kids of Dunster Institute actually even get the point of "The Honorary Shepherds" when they see it on Student Display Night. They clap politely. But Lee and Pete have both learned something. Ms. Cabbage has taught them well.

A myth is yours only if you choose to own it.

Myths, like faith, are wide and capacious and of their nature generous.

There is more that she teaches them, but it can't all be put into words. They put it on their lips and give it to each other from time to time, and in this way they remember her after she dies.

GREGORY MAGUIRE

I was born and raised in Albany, New York, and went to high school and college there too. Not far from Albany in three directions are mountain ranges—the Adirondacks to the north, the Berkshires and Green Mountains to the east, and the Helderbergs and Catskills to the south. The edge of my horizon has always been mountain ringed, in dream and abstraction if not in fact, and an urge to be the bear who went over the mountain "to see what he could see" has led me to travel a good deal. I lived for some years in Cambridge and Boston, took my doctorate at Tufts University, and write this from my home in London, which is not my final home (I trust) but suitably exciting and within a day's air travel of mountains yet unsighted and tempting.

I began to write when I was a child. All stories are journeys. My current books include *Missing Sisters*, my first genuinely "realistic" novel, and *Seven Spiders Spinning*, a spoof of horror-story conventions.

Writing "The Honorary Shepherds" was for me another kind of journey, one I was eager to take. I've had dear friends die of AIDS, and I've watched them struggle—often successfully—to derive comfort from their families and the larger "families" of faith, ethnicity, and culture from which they sprang. "The Honorary Shepherds" isn't a story about AIDS per se, but it is born of a conviction: As individuals have the power to break away from their origins, so they also possess the power to maintain and strengthen the ties that nourish them.

RUNNING

by Ellen Howard

I'm *bringing someone* with me, Terry," my stepsister, Heather, was saying through the crackle of the long-distance telephone connection. I had to listen hard to make sense out of the garbled sound of her voice. "A friend," I think she said, and then something like, "Do me a favor, will you, and kind of prepare Mama and Art." Prepare them for what? I wondered, and Heather's next words didn't make it any clearer. "Sheila's nice, but she's . . . well, she's got some problems," she was saying. "She needs to be with a family like ours that's a little goose."

"Goose?" I shouted into the receiver. I wished Dad or my stepmom, Irene, were home to take this call. Somehow, I always seemed to get stuck carrying Heather's crazy messages. "Talk a little slower, Heather," I yelled at her. "I thought you said a little *goose.*"

"Loose!" she shouted back, and kept right on talking a mile a minute. "You know, not uptight! She's had some trouble with her folks. . . . I'll explain when we get

87

there. Our plane comes in at O'Hare. Write this down, will you, and Terry . . . get it right!"

So that's how Sheila came into my life. She was supposed to be *Heather's* friend.

Irene was real excited when I gave her the news that night at dinner that Heather was on her way home from Europe. The trip had been a high school graduation gift from Heather's dad, who's got the bucks to do that sort of showy, spectacular thing. You could tell Irene felt all mixed up about it—glad that Heather could have the trip, but wishing she and my dad could have been the ones to give it, and worried to have her only born daughter trotting around foreign countries without her. Well, she'd have to get used to Heather being gone, I figured. Next fall it was college for Heather, and Irene would have only me left at home to fuss over. Neither of us was particularly thrilled at that prospect, I imagined.

"Oh, by the way," I said when Irene had calmed down a little. "Heather said to tell you she's bringing a friend home with her."

Irene looked up, startled. I saw her eyes meet Dad's fleetingly over the dinner table and then drill into me.

"A friend?" she said.

"Yeah. Said she was having some kind of trouble with her family, and Heather thought she could stay with us for a while."

"Oh, a *girl* friend," Irene said.

I could see she was relieved. Irene probably wasn't wild about the idea of Heather getting too involved with a boy right then. She had a scholarship, and I suppose Irene didn't want her to louse it up.

Go figure parents! They worried about Heather because she *might* have a boyfriend, and they worried about me because I *didn't*.

I don't know how *I* felt about Heather coming home, or bringing a friend. Actually, I don't think I was feeling much of anything just then. Except a blank kind of misery. I didn't know why. And anger. I seemed to be mad all the time, but again I couldn't have told you why. I just was . . . I don't know . . . lonely, I guess. Dad and Irene had each other. Heather always had some sort of boyfriend or other. I looked around, and it seemed as though everyone had someone. Even Maggie, my very best friend since preschool, had gotten a boyfriend just before school let out for the summer. I don't know what it is about boys that makes girls act the way they do. Suddenly all she could talk about was Kevin. She was as silly and disgusting as the girls we used to laugh at together.

"You just wait, Terr, until it happens to you," she had told me. "Then you'll understand."

But I knew I wouldn't. I never would understand how a person who had been your best friend practically your whole life could just drop you. Suddenly, no matter what Maggie and I might have planned, if Kevin called, our plans were off.

"He has to come first with me," Maggie said. "He just has

to. I still like you, Terr. I really do. You're still my best friend. But Kevin's my *boyfriend*!"

Maybe that's why I found myself feeling so glad to see Heather plodding up the ramp from the airport gate.

She was, after all, my only sister. Ever since Dad and Irene got married when we were little kids, Heather and I had been together, playing and fighting and laughing and crying together. Good old Heather! I thought when I caught sight of her.

She looked just the same—long straight hair straggling down her back and an outfit that looked like it came from Goodwill. Europe hadn't changed her a bit. I craned my neck for her friend. Heather's friends always looked like refugees from the sixties, just like she did. But all I saw was a small, pretty girl in khaki slacks and shirt, with a short curly haircut. I glanced at her and decided *she* couldn't be the one. She looked like she didn't have a problem in the world.

Irene and Heather were hugging and laughing, and Heather was talking a blue streak, the way Heather does. Then Dad got a hug, and so did I, and then we realized that people were having to elbow their ways around us because we were standing in the middle of the exit. So Dad shooed us over against a wall. The pretty girl came too.

"Sheila," Heather was babbling, "this is my mother, Irene Jackson, and my stepdad, Art, and my stepsis, Terry."

The girl put out her hand and shook all around.

"Pleased to meet you," she said. She had an accent I couldn't place—though it wasn't European, a subject we had speculated on. Her hand was hot and dry and strong. Something about the way she looked at me made me blush, and I felt my heart lurch.

"Uh, nice to know you," I stammered, and then turned away, feeling embarrassed and confused for no reason I could think of. "Hey, I'm starved," I blustered. "Let' s go home."

Sheila O'Flaherty was from the East Coast. Heather had met her in the youth hostel where they were both staying in London. Sheila was looking for some way to avoid going home, since her folks had apparently told her "never to darken their doorway again," or something equally dramatic, and Heather was, we gathered, nursing a mega case of homesickness.

Heather has never been able to resist a sob story—"She's a born social worker," Dad says. She decided that what Sheila needed was a new start in life, with us as her sponsors. That's another thing Heather is good at—deciding what other people ought to do. Since she was looking for an excuse to come home early anyway, she stayed behind when her group moved on. Then she and Sheila pooled their resources and booked two cut-rate student tickets back to the States.

"Her folks must be really ignorant, turning on her like that," Heather told us a couple of days later, when Sheila was out and we could talk. Heather had conned her old boyfriend George into taking Sheila to meet his sister, who was looking for a baby-sitter. Like I said, Heather's good at arranging other people's lives.

"She isn't . . . pregnant, is she?" Irene wanted to know.

"Or some kind of delinquent?" That was Dad.

"No, no." Heather laughed. "It's just that she likes women."

"Likes women?"

"You know. She's gay. Lesbian. Whatever you want to call it. She likes women instead of men, and when her folks found out, they had a fit. She feels awful about it. She knew they wouldn't be overjoyed, but she never dreamed they'd not even want to see her again. What a couple of creeps!"

Irene and Dad were glancing at one another, the color drained from their faces. Irene licked her lips.

"Uh, Heather, honey . . . you two aren't . . . you know, you aren't . . . "

"Lovers?" Heather let out a hoot and rocked back against her chair. "Mama, you've got to be kidding. Old man-crazy me? *I* don't know what she sees in women, but, hey . . . She certainly didn't *choose* to be that way. As she tells it, she couldn't even admit it to herself for the longest time. But she is, and I think it's rotten that her parents are behaving the way they are. Her father's a college professor. You'd think he'd know better, but I gather they're some kind of religious nuts. Well, not nuts exactly, but anyway really into their religion, which says homosexuality's a sin. That makes Sheila a sinner, I guess."

"Poor child," Irene said, sighing.

Suddenly she was all sympathy, I noticed, as soon as her precious Heather proved to be untainted.

"Hey, you guys don't mind her staying here for a while, do you?" Heather asked, a little belatedly, it seemed to me.

"Of course not," Dad said, but I could see that he was uncomfortable.

Dad and Irene like to think they're extremely liberal and modern and unprejudiced, but it was pretty clear to me that they didn't always *feel* the tolerance they mouthed. And in this case I couldn't blame them. After all, if what Heather said was true, Sheila was a *queer*. It made me feel funny too, thinking about one of *them* in my very own house.

Still, no one was asking *me* what I thought. They never did. In these kinds of conversations, no one ever turned to ask, "Terry, what do *you* think?" They seemed to assume that just because I was there, listening, I was somehow *involved*.

The thing was, now that I knew about Sheila, I found myself thinking about her all the time, and feeling . . . well, *confused*. For one thing, I always thought that lesbians looked like dykes. You know, rough-talking and crude-looking, with butch haircuts and leather jackets and real hard faces. But Sheila . . . Sheila wasn't like that at all. She didn't seem any different from anyone else, except for being an Easterner, of course, and that was sort of interesting— the clipped rhythm of her voice, her Easterner's expressions. And she *was* pretty. One of the prettiest girls I'd ever seen, with soft-looking skin and shadowed eyes and a cloud of short, dark hair. She seemed . . . well, feminine. That was what really got me. In many ways, she seemed more feminine than me!

Still, I decided to keep my distance. I didn't want her coming on to me, for heaven's sake!

▼

Sheila got the baby-sitting job with George's sister's kids. Heather was obsessed with sorting her stuff and packing up for college and saying endless good-byes to friends who were going to different schools. Dad and Irene were away at work all day. Maggie was—you guessed it—with *Kevin* practically every waking moment.

I slept a lot, ran on the high school track every morning, practiced layups at the hoop in the park, mostly hung out. I was so successful at avoiding Sheila that I rarely saw her, even though we were living in the same house; and for some reason *that* made me sadder and lonelier than before. My trouble was I had too much time to think. I even began— don't laugh—to wish school would start again, just to get my mind off things.

But first, the end of August, would be basketball camp. That, at least, was something to look forward to. Maggie and I had been going every summer since junior high. We were, after all, the stars of our team. No one could dribble and pass the way Maggie could, and no one could shoot it into the basket as sweetly as me.

Basketball camp would be long days of showing our stuff to other girls who were practically as good as we were, and long evenings of talking and joking around the way we used to. Maggie had always cracked me up! Once, last summer, we got one of the older girls to buy us some beer, and Maggie ended up astride the cannon in Bronson Park, singing at the top of her lungs . . . until I hauled her off and dunked her in the fountain.

94

▼

The way the rest of the summer had gone, I suppose I shouldn't have been surprised when Maggie called—she didn't even have the guts to come tell me in person. But I was. Surprised and madder than I'd ever been.

"What do you mean you aren't going?" I yelled.

"Ter-*ry* . . ." Maggie's voice was cajoling. "You know how it is. Kevin—"

"Kevin! What's he got to do—"

"He's asked me to his folks' cabin at the lake. I just *have* to go."

I tried to keep my voice from shaking.

"You don't *have* to do anything, Mag."

There was a silence. Then, quietly, came Maggie's voice.

"No, I don't have to. I *want* to, Terry."

"More than you want to go to camp with me?"

Again a silence.

"Terry, I don't want to hurt your feelings. You know I love you like a sister, but . . ."

Even I could hear the bitterness in my voice.

"But Kevin's your *boyfriend*."

"Yes. Yes, he is. And if you'd grow up and find a boyfriend of your own, you'd understand. I mean, come on, Terry! Plenty of guys have been interested. You know they have. But you never give them the time of day. We're not kids anymore, Terry. We're going to be seniors next year. Almost *women*. And women like men. I like men. Everybody does, except—"

I slammed down the receiver.

I didn't have to take that. Not even from Maggie. And, besides, it wasn't true. I *liked* boys. Only I didn't put them ahead of my best friend. I had some sense of loyalty, some . . .

I punched the wall over the desk, unable to hold back any longer, and felt the crashing pain in my knuckles that released my tears.

It was that moment that Sheila chose to come into the room.

I could feel her looking at me, feel her gray eyes taking it all in, my red face and runny nose and the way I was cradling my swelling hand and the ugly sobs I couldn't keep back. But I couldn't look at her. I tried to shove past her to run upstairs, but felt her firm restraining hand on my shoulder and heard her voice, brisk and businesslike.

"What you need, Terry, my girl," Sheila said, "is a nice cup of tea."

I don't even *like* tea, but somehow I found myself sitting on a stool at the kitchen counter, watching Sheila pour boiling water into a teapot.

She was talking about the kids she baby-sat, I realized—the Kemp kids. They were real little monsters, she said, but funny and kind of fascinating.

"Trying to figure out what's going on in their strange little brains, that's the trick," she was saying. She hadn't asked me what was wrong, had only handed me a tissue and steered me to the stool and started talking.

"Actually, that's what I've been doing all my life," she was saying, "trying to figure out what's going on in other people's heads. It seems to be so different so much of the time from what's going on in mine. . . ."

She let the sentence sort of hang there in the air. So different . . . I'd been wrong, I thought. She *was* different from other people. Even if I hadn't known about . . . about her being . . . what she was, eventually I'd have seen she was different from any girl I'd known. And I *liked* her difference, I found myself thinking. I liked it a lot.

I looked at her for the first time since she'd barged in on me. She was gazing intently at her watch, really serious about the way she made tea, timing it to the second. Not like me, I thought, who never timed anything, not even a three-minute egg. So why did I feel . . . I don't know . . . that we were *alike* somehow? That she knew what I was feeling, even though I hadn't told her, even though I was all sweaty and bleary and really steamed at Maggie, and she seemed so cool, so tranquil, pouring out two cups of tea.

"*I* don't care what other people are thinking," I said, taking the cup from her and feeling again the strong, dry heat of her hand against mine.

She picked up her own cup and sipped tentatively.

"Careful," she said. "Don't burn yourself."

And for some silly reason I felt the tears start behind my eyes again. I ducked my head over my cup, wishing she'd put her arm around me again the way she had when she steered me into the kitchen.

▼

I don't know what people who don't exercise *do* about their feelings. How else can you keep from exploding, except to run until you feel empty or pump iron until you've sweated out the pain inside and exchanged it for aching muscles?

That was what I was doing early the next morning after an almost sleepless night—pounding out my feelings on the smooth, black high school track. I had finally hit my stride, my breathing smoothed, my pace easy, and my mind emptied of the turmoil of the night, when I realized that the runner ahead of me—the one whose loose, long-legged stride I was admiring—was Sheila. She had the hood of her sweatshirt up—mornings were cool this early—so maybe that's why I hadn't recognized her at first, but suddenly I was faltering, gulping for air. For a moment I was tempted to sprint away, and then I took a steadying breath, shook my hair back, and put on a spurt of speed forward. By the time I came up even with her, the heat in my face was fading. My voice sounded cool enough when I said, "Hi."

Sheila looked over, and I noticed she missed a step.

"Hi," she said, recovering her stride.

We ran like that, side by side, for several minutes without talking. I remember thinking it was strange that our strides matched so perfectly. Sheila was a head shorter than me and slim where I'm stocky. It must have been those long legs of hers. She matched me step for step.

"I didn't know you were into running," I said, trying to keep the breathlessness out of my voice.

"Sometimes."

"I come here every morning," I said. "I've never seen you before."

She didn't answer, and we ran, perfectly in pace.

"Hey, Sheila," I said. "Thanks for . . . for yesterday."

She shrugged and slowed to a walk, swinging her arms and still lifting her legs. I slowed too.

"My friend," I said, wanting to explain, wanting her to know, "my friend had just called to say she wasn't going to basketball camp with me. Her boyfriend invited her to his lake cabin."

"Ah," said Sheila.

"It made me mad," I said.

"And sad?"

I started to say no, and then I stopped.

She nodded, catching my eye and holding it.

"I know," she said softly. Suddenly, I knew that she did.

We had stopped running. Two racewalkers shouldered past us on the track.

Sheila stepped off into the grass, and I followed her.

"Time to be getting back," she said. "The Kemp kids awaiteth."

I fell into step beside her.

"What sports do you play?" I asked, for something to break the silence.

"Me? None. I've got the grace and coordination of a tree sloth."

"You're a *good* runner," I said.

"Well that's not sports, is it? You don't have to compete against anyone, except yourself. I can keep up with *me*."

"No, really," I said, suddenly intense. "I was watching you. I bet you could go out for track easy."

Sheila flashed me her wonderful smile.

"Thanks. There aren't too many track teams in secretarial school."

"Secretarial school?"

"If I can manage it," she said. "I've got to learn fast how to do something to earn a living. I've used up my travel money, and I can't live off the generosity of your parents forever, now can I?"

I shook my head. I had hardly noticed where we were going, but there, up ahead, was our house.

"You're baby-sitting," I said, stupidly.

Sheila laughed, but the laugh had a bitter edge to it.

"You can't *live* on what I earn, Terry. Not that I'm not grateful to Heather and her friend for finding me the job."

"Well, but can't your fo—" I broke off, remembering what Heather had said about Sheila's folks. No, I guess they wouldn't send her money for college. I'd just assumed she was going. The thing was, I suddenly realized, I'd been so wrapped up in my own misery, I hadn't given a thought to what Sheila must be feeling so far away from home—about her folks, about what was going to happen to her now that she'd "come out," as Heather called it.

"So, in the fall, you're going to secretarial school?" I said.

We were walking up our driveway, toward the front door. She nodded.

"Well, I'm sure that's interesting work." It was a dumb

remark, but all I could think of to say.

"*I'm* not sure," she said, "but it seems to be my only option. . . ." Her voice trembled and faded away. She had reached for the door handle.

"Sheila," I said, "I didn't realize. I . . . I'm sorry."

She stood for a moment, her head bowed over the door handle. Then she put back her shoulders, lifted her head, and turned to face me.

"Don't be, Terry," she said. "Secretarial school is nothing—just something I have to do for a while. Even my folks . . . It's shitty of them to throw me out on my ear just because, for the first time in my life, I've been honest with them But the important thing is I *have* been honest—with them, and most of all with myself. I'm who I am, and I like who I am. . . ."

I just stood there, looking at her. I could see that it was true. She wasn't ashamed. The things that made her unhappy were all outside herself, nothing to do with who she was inside.

She put her hand on my arm, and once again I felt her touch at my center. She seemed to be looking right into me, and suddenly she wasn't talking about herself.

"You're going to have to deal with it, Terry," she said.

I knew she didn't mean my having to go to camp without Maggie.

And then she had slipped through the door, leaving me outside. But the door was open. If I had the courage, I could follow.

ELLEN HOWARD

As a writer I'm something of a late bloomer. My career began with the acceptance of my first novel, *Circle of Giving*, on my fortieth birthday. That book received the Golden Kite Honor Book Award for 1984.

Since then I have published eleven books, ranging from a historical novel, *When Daylight Comes*, about a slave rebellion in the Caribbean in 1733, to a contemporary novel, *Gillyflower*, that deals with child sexual abuse. Both those books, as well as *Her Own Song*, about adoption and racial prejudice, were named Notable Children's Trade Books in Social Studies, and *Gillyflower* has been translated into six foreign languages. Several of my books are drawn from stories of my grandmother's rural Midwestern family. Of these, *Edith Herself*, a *School Library Journal* Best Book, has proven very popular with young readers, and *Sister* was named an American Library Association Notable Children's Book.

Although I have lived most of my life in Oregon, my husband, Chuck, and I moved to Kalamazoo, Michigan, in 1990. We are the parents of four grown daughters, one of whom, Shaley, is a lesbian.

Of all my failings as a parent, I most regret my lack of support for Shaley in her struggle to find her lesbian identity. I was "running" from the knowledge of her lesbianism, just as the character in my story is running—not because lesbianism is shameful, but because, in our society, it takes great courage to lead a lesbian lifestyle. I am happy to be able to say that, despite my cowardice, our daughter has found that courage.

THREE
MONDAYS IN
JULY

▽

by James Cross Giblin

*S*ummer *1951. No Walkmans. No VCRs. Television was still a novelty, and not many homes had sets. It was before the Beatles, even before Elvis. The word "gay" meant "merry; happy; light-hearted" according to* Webster's. *If people talked about homosexuals—which they rarely did; homosexuality was virtually a forbidden topic—they called them "queers," "fairies," "dykes," or more politely, "deviates." But in big cities and small towns across America, there were many young men and women who found themselves responding to members of their own sex. . . .*

"Could you come here a minute, David?" It was his mother calling from the kitchen, and she didn't sound as if she would take no for an answer.

David turned away from his bedroom window, which faced the street. "Be right there as soon as I finish making my bed," he called back. He pulled the bottom sheet tight before looking out the window again.

Across the street a boy David didn't know was mowing old Mrs. Herendeen's lawn. The boy looked older than David— maybe eighteen—and he was certainly stockier. He had removed his shirt on this sticky July afternoon, and the sunlight slanting between the maple leaves highlighted the muscles in his broad back.

David felt perspiration break out on his forehead as he watched the boy. The air was close in the bedroom, but David knew that wasn't the reason for his sudden warmth. He remembered the summer before, when another boy had mowed Mrs. Herendeen's lawn and clipped her hedges, and David—watching from the privacy of the spare-bedroom window upstairs—had felt heat rise in his body and had begun to fondle himself.

Enough of that. David forced his gaze away from the window and drew the chenille spread up over the narrow bed. This was a different summer, and it had been a long time since he'd retreated to the room upstairs—supposedly to look through the old books and magazines that were stored there. Now he had his driver's license and a full-time summer job at the library. The same urges still rose in him—fiercely, unpredictably—but it was easier to subdue them. Most of the time.

David didn't know why he responded so strongly to the sight of the male body; he simply did, and had as far back as he could remember. What he did know, from things he'd read and remarks overheard at school, was that most people thought such feelings were shameful, even evil. So he tried his best to suppress them.

Finishing with the bed, David left his room, crossed a corner of the dining room, and entered the kitchen. In their hundred-year-old house, most of the rooms were on the ground floor.

"Well, that took you long enough," his mother said. She finished drying the last of the lunch plates and set it on the stack in the cupboard.

"I stopped to read Paul's postcard again," David said. Paul was David's best friend, off on a vacation trip in New England with his family.

His mother gave David a quizzical look, as if she sensed he wasn't telling her the truth. It made him wonder again how much she knew about his fantasies, his secrets. Had she guessed why he used to spend so much time upstairs?

"I'll bet I know what you want me to do," he said, hoping to lighten the mood and gain the initiative.

"Oh, you do?" She brushed a loose strand of gray hair back in place.

"Weed the rock garden, right?"

"You must have read my mind." She smiled.

Good, David thought. Now he might have a chance to do what he really wanted that afternoon. "First, though, I'd like to drive over to the beach for a while," he said.

Her smile started to fade.

"Don't worry. I'll only be gone an hour or so. I promise."

At that point another son might have hugged his mother to reinforce his vow. But neither David nor his mother were huggers. Instead, they simply stood there in the kitchen looking at one another in a quiet contest of wills.

David won. "Well, all right," his mother said. "After all, it is your day off from the library. And it would probably be better to do the weeding later, when the sun isn't so high in the sky." She smiled again. "We wouldn't want you getting a sunstroke."

The low-lying shore of Lake Erie was just two miles from David's home in the suburban town of Sainsbury, named for a pioneer settler in northeastern Ohio. As David drove past small farms with stands displaying home-grown tomatoes, he relaxed in the driver's seat. Traffic was light, so he could afford to let his mind wander.

There was no radio in the Ford two-door, but David didn't mind. He was just glad they lived so close to town that his father could walk to and from his law office. Otherwise, David wouldn't have had the use of the family car on these summer afternoons.

David slowed as a yellow cat streaked across the country road. He wondered what his friend Paul was doing at that moment. He'd be in Boston now, staying with his grandparents. And if David knew Paul, he'd be trying to get out of some sightseeing trip so that he could go to a first-run movie at one of the big downtown theaters.

"You've got to see *A Place in the Sun*," Paul had written on the postcard he'd sent from Northampton. "The closeups of Elizabeth Taylor and Montgomery Clift are just incredible!"

David had never had a friend like Paul. In fact, until Paul turned up in his homeroom last fall, David had never known another boy who shared his love for movies, books, and plays. He'd thought he was the only one in Sainsbury who kept up with the Broadway theater by reading the Sunday *New York Times*.

A pair of gulls flew low over the marsh on the left side of the road. It wasn't far to the beach from there. If Paul were with him now, David thought, they'd be planning an expedition to Cleveland to see the new French movie that had just opened. Or they'd be discussing Henry James's story *Washington Square*, which they'd both read after seeing the film version, *The Heiress*. But they wouldn't be talking about anything more personal. They never did.

Paul and he shared so many interests that David often wondered if his wiry, dark-haired friend shared some of the same fantasies, too. Lying in bed alone at night, did Paul, like David, visualize male bodies—sometimes those of movie stars like Tyrone Power, sometimes those of muscular boys he knew? But David had never had the courage to hint at the subject, let alone bring it up directly.

Ahead on the right loomed the gate to the state park. As David turned off the paved highway, waves of dust rose from the dirt road that led to the beach. The trees on either side gave way to scraggly bushes, and then the lake came into view, its calm surface glimmering in the midafternoon light.

Since it was Monday, there weren't many cars in the parking lot. David found a good spot in one of the few shady patches. Before getting out of the car, he slipped off his loafers and socks and rolled up his khaki slacks. He hadn't brought

111

a beach towel because he didn't plan to stretch out on the sand. And he didn't intend to go into the water because he'd never learned how to swim. Instead he'd do what he most enjoyed—walk past the concession stand and the section near the parking lot where most people clustered, and explore the dunes at the far end of the beach.

He started out along the road—a dirt track, really—that skirted the back of the beach. Before long he passed the last of the sunbathers and swimmers. Now the beach was marked by clumps of grass and piles of small rocks. Here David could walk alone and daydream about the roles he would act on the stage one day, about the great plays he would write. He had already begun to get leading parts in the drama-club productions at school.

The dirt track narrowed further. A stand of poplars loomed on David's right, and beyond them the sand rose and fell in a series of dunes. He left the track and had started toward the dunes when a sudden movement caught his eye. He stopped behind one of the trees and peered around it. Who could be there? No one ever came to this part of the beach.

While David watched, a man slowly rose from the hollow between two dunes. He stood with hands on hips and stared out at the lake. The man had his back to David, and the sun glistened from the beginning of a bald spot on top of his head.

Although it sported a nut-brown tan, the man's body was far from perfect. His shoulders sloped and his long arms were lightly muscled. Even so, David felt his heart beat more rapidly as he watched him. For the man was wearing snug

112

black swim trunks—the briefest trunks David had ever seen except on actors in Italian movies.

The man glanced to his left and then to the right, but did not turn around. If he had, he would almost certainly have seen David. The man took off his wristwatch and knelt in the hollow to put it away. David could just make out the top of a beach bag. Then the man strode down to the shore—deserted at this point—and walked straight into the water.

David hunkered down on the ground behind the tree and kept his gaze fixed on the man's head in the water. From that distance it looked like a dark ball bobbing up and down on the surface. David's right calf began to cramp and he could feel sweat gathering behind his knees. But he did not change position. If anyone had asked him what he was waiting for, he could not have answered. All he knew was that he felt compelled to wait and watch.

After what seemed like an hour but was probably no more than twenty minutes, the man emerged from the water. He slicked back his thinning hair and then walked slowly, deliberately toward the hollow.

David made himself as small as possible behind the tree and studied the man. A coating of gray-black hair covered his chest, and his wet trunks seemed even briefer than before. David felt a wave of heat spread up through his body, and it alarmed him. Why was he so fascinated by this stranger?

The man had reached the hollow by now and was rubbing himself down with an aqua beach towel. Finishing, he looked to left and right once more as if to make sure he was alone.

And then, as David stared unbelievingly, the man rolled his trunks down over his hips and stepped out of them.

David's breath caught in his chest. Other than the guys in gym class, he had never seen a naked man before—not even his father. And he certainly never imagined he would see one on a public beach. He felt as if he should avert his gaze and focus on something else—the gnarled branches of a shrub or the small white blossoms on a wildflower. But he could not make himself look at anything except the man's bronzed body.

The man turned then and prepared to stretch out on the towel. David tried to back away before the man could see him, but his awkward movement attracted the man's attention. "What the hell?" he exclaimed.

David scrambled to his feet, and for a moment his gaze locked with the man's startled brown eyes. Then, without saying anything, David walked stiffly away along the dirt road. He thought the man might call after him, stop him—he almost hoped he would. However, no words came as David put more distance between himself and the hollow.

The afternoon sun beat down on his head, but something else was making his face flush. He felt guilty, as if he'd been caught doing something terrible. But what exactly?

When he reached another stand of trees, he stopped and looked back toward the dunes. There was no sign of the man. Had he packed up his gear and gone in the opposite direction while David had been walking? Or was he stretched out on his towel in the hollow? David felt his breath catch again as he imagined the second possibility, and for a moment he thought of retracing his steps to find out.

Don't be a fool, he said to himself. You were embarrassed once; do you want to be embarrassed again? He swung around and headed in the opposite direction, toward the parking lot. He'd told his mother he wouldn't be gone more than an hour, and an hour and a half had passed already.

David crossed the parking lot, unlocked the car, and put on his loafers. The tops of his feet stung; he'd probably be sunburned there tomorrow. As he started the engine, he thought again of the man in the hollow. Did he come there often? Would he be there next Monday? Would he—?

No, I mustn't think about that, David told himself angrily. With a screech of tires he backed out of the parking space and turned toward home.

"Where are you off to this afternoon?" his mother asked. It was the following Monday and she was sitting in the living room, reading a biography of Marie Antoinette.

"I thought I'd go back to the beach," David replied from the doorway. He kept his voice low and casual; if his mother saw how eager he was to return, she'd be sure to wonder why.

She smiled fondly at him. "Well, have a good time. But don't stay in the sun too long. You know how easily you burn." Having offered that bit of maternal advice, she opened her book once more.

As he got into the car, David found himself wishing he weren't an only child. Then maybe his mother wouldn't be so concerned about him. But he had to admit that her concern was preferable to his father's seeming lack of interest most of the time. At least his mother appeared to have some idea of who he was.

He drove faster than usual, impatient to get to the beach and see if the man was there. All week long—while he'd been putting books back on the shelves at the library, or mowing the backyard, or lying in his bed at night—visions of the man had flashed suddenly, unexpectedly into his thoughts. Over and over he saw the man's back, watched him swim, and held his breath as the man slowly removed his trunks.

The visions troubled David, and he tried to stop them, to think of other things. But they only returned, more insistently than before. Now they were impelling him back to the beach in hopes of—what? What did he want from the man? David honestly didn't know.

In the parking lot, after slipping out of his loafers, David also pulled off his slacks. Today he had put on his baggy blue gym shorts under them. He was almost running by the time he started down the dirt track toward the dunes, and forced himself to slow down. Up ahead he saw the hollow. Would the man be there?

Cautiously David approached the stand of trees from which he'd watched the man the week before. He bent down and moved slowly, soundlessly, as if he were on a reconnaissance mission. Well, in a way I am, he thought.

He positioned himself behind a tree and looked out at the hollow. There was no movement there, no sign of life. He scanned the dunes on either side and the lake ahead. Nothing there, either—no strollers on the sand, no swimmers in the water.

He sat back. Maybe the man hadn't arrived yet. Or maybe he was stretched out at the bottom of the hollow, sunning himself. Would he be wearing the black bikini, or lying there in the nude? David felt his forehead grow hot as he visualized the scene.

He waited. He waited some more. Gulls screeched overhead. A bee buzzed around a clump of beach clover. David shifted position, but it didn't help much. His scalp prickled from the heat, and his legs began to ache.

At last he stood up. Checking his watch, he was surprised to see that forty minutes had passed. If the man was in the hollow, he surely would have moved by now. But David felt compelled to check, to see for himself.

Boldness seemed the best course of action. He wouldn't sneak up on the hollow; instead he'd walk straight up to it, and if the man were there, David would act as if he were simply heading down to the water. Feeling more confident, he left the security of the trees and set out between the dunes.

The hollow was empty. David ached with disappointment—a disappointment so fierce that he almost felt like crying. He had so much wanted the man to be there.

Why? He still didn't know. It wasn't that the man was handsome, because he wasn't—not really. And he wasn't young either. No, David's fascination with him stemmed from something else—a mysterious and powerful force that David had never experienced before. Not with the boys he'd watched from a window, not with Paul, not with anyone.

For a moment he stretched out full length in the hollow and stared at a cloud that was passing over the sun. Instead of a lanky boy in a wrinkled shirt and baggy shorts, David imagined what it would be like to be the man, lying there in his sleek bikini. . . .

The fantasy was alarming, and David stood up quickly before it got the better of him. The beach was no place to fool around. What if someone should see him?

Itching with frustration, David returned to the dirt track and headed for the parking lot. He looked back once at the hollow, but of course no one was there.

When David woke up the following Monday, dark clouds hung low in the sky, and it looked as if it might rain any minute. Damn. Even though the man hadn't showed up the week before, David had convinced himself that he'd be on the beach today. But he certainly wouldn't come if it was raining.

At breakfast David snapped at his mother when she asked him if he wanted jam on his toast. Afterward, to make up, he volunteered to weed the flower beds.

"Why don't you wait and see if it rains?" she said.

"No, I'll do it now." Anything would be better than sitting around the house on this gloomy day.

"But maybe the sun will come out later."

"If it does, I want to go to the beach!" David's voice was louder than he intended, and he looked quickly to see if his mother had picked up on his agitation. The last thing he needed was for her to start asking questions about the beach and what he did there.

She merely poured herself another cup of coffee and said, "Well, let's hope you get what you want."

The sun broke through the clouds a little before lunch, and David set out for the beach as soon as he could afterward. Once he was in the car, he unbuttoned the top two buttons on his sport shirt. The hot breeze blowing through the window felt good on his exposed chest.

When David reached the screen of trees on the beach, he looked toward the hollow. There was no sign of the man, but David felt oddly unconcerned. For some reason he couldn't have explained, he was sure he'd see the man again that day.

He unfolded the large bath towel he had brought with him and spread it on the sand in front of the trees. Their fluttering leaves partially shielded him from the sun after he stretched out on the towel. He unbuttoned the rest of the buttons on his shirt but didn't take it off. Why risk getting a burn on his chest and shoulders?

He didn't know how long he'd dozed when the sting of a sand fly awakened him. Brushing it away from his neck, he looked about dazedly and saw the man standing in the hollow. He was wearing the same black bikini as before, and he was looking in David's direction.

Suddenly shy, David lowered his gaze. When he raised his eyes again, the man had turned away and was rubbing suntan lotion on his arms. That done, he knelt down in the hollow and disappeared from view.

David rose to his haunches on the towel and sat there, hugging his knees and staring in the direction of the hollow. As the minutes passed, he lost all sense of time. He longed to make a move, but where could he go? He didn't want to retreat to the trees and he was afraid to move closer to the man. His entire being seemed to be concentrated on waiting, waiting. . . .

At last, almost as if willed by David, the man raised himself on his elbows and looked over the rim of the hollow. "What do you want, kid?" he asked abruptly. "Why are you spying on me?"

"I wasn't spying," David said. "I just—"

"Just what?"

"I—I—" David couldn't stop stammering.

The man stood up and brushed sand off his legs. "I hope you didn't tell anyone you saw me sunbathing in the nude," he said. "You know I could get arrested for that."

"No—no, of course I didn't!" David hugged his knees tighter. What did the man think he was? Besides, whom would he tell?

The man seemed to sense his discomfort. He walked over to David's towel and crouched down near him. When he spoke again, his voice was softer. "I'm sorry. I didn't mean to accuse you of anything," he said. "It's just that I'm a stranger around here, and I don't know what's safe—and what isn't."

"You surprised me, that's all," David said. "I'd never seen anyone take off his trunks on the beach before."

As soon as the words were out of his mouth, David realized how silly they must sound. But the man simply smiled. "Don't tell me you were turned on by seeing an old guy like me bare-assed."

"You're not old!" David exclaimed.

"Thanks, kid, but I'm thirty-eight. And that's a hell of a lot older than you."

"I'll be seventeen next month," David said defensively. Without meaning to, he found himself staring at the man's form-fitting trunks. He might as well be naked now, considering how little of his body the trunks concealed.

Embarrassed by his own thought, David looked quickly away. But the man knew what was going on. "That's okay," he said gently.

"Okay?" David's voice quivered.

"You can look at my body all you want. I'm flattered."

David let out a great sigh. He hadn't realized he'd been holding his breath.

"You've got a good body yourself," the man said. "From what I can see of it."

A good body? No one had ever told David that before. He himself thought his arms were too spindly, his chest too thin. But if this man said . . .

David turned to him and examined his face more closely. After all, the man had given him permission to do so. He noticed the smile lines—or were they lines of worry?—around his eyes and the dimple in his chin.

The man returned David's gaze directly and then stood up.

121

What would happen next? David wondered. Would the man reach out to him, touch him? Would he suggest that they drive someplace where they could be alone, the way actors did in movies? David had no real notion what might transpire, but his skin tingled with a mixture of excitement and fear.

"It's hot back here by the trees," the man said. He swatted a sand fly that was biting his arm. "What say we take a walk down by the water?"

A vague disappointment replaced his earlier excitement as David stood up also. There was no privacy down by the water.

Again, the man seemed to sense what David was thinking. He touched his shoulder lightly, sending a shiver down David's arm. "I think I know what you want, kid—what you've been hoping for," he said.

"I haven't been hoping for anything!—" David started to protest. He felt as if the man had suddenly stripped him bare.

"I know, I know," the man said. "But this isn't the right place—and I'm not the right person." He went on quickly, before David could interrupt. "That doesn't mean I don't like you and think you're handsome, because I do."

Handsome? Had David heard him correctly?

"But I have to leave soon," the man was saying. "So do you want to go for that walk or not?"

David nodded.

"By the way, my name's Allen. What's yours?"

"David."

"Glad to meet you, David." The man shook his hand, really

gripped it. David could not remember ever receiving such a firm handshake.

For the next half hour David and Allen strolled along the lakeshore. They waded in the cool, shallow water and tried to see who could skim stones the farthest on the lake's placid surface.

David learned that Allen was the buyer for the men's-wear department of a big store in Chicago. That explained the bikini—he'd picked it up on a buying trip to Italy. Allen had come to Sainsbury to visit his aunt and uncle. He was returning to Chicago the next day.

David, in turn, told Allen about his life. He talked of his aging parents and his friend Paul, and confided his dreams of a career in the theater.

Trusting this man who had so recently been a stranger, David went on to tell Allen secret things he'd never told anyone before. He acknowledged that he was a virgin. And, speaking in a whisper although there was no one else nearby, he told him how fascinated he was by the look and shape of men's bodies.

The sun was low in the afternoon sky when Allen skimmed a final stone across the water and turned to David. "I've got to go now," he said.

They returned to the hollow and Allen gathered his things. Even though he knew the answer, David asked the question anyway: "You won't be here next Monday, will you?"

"No, I'll be back on the job in Chicago." Allen reached out and clasped David's shoulders. "But why don't you come anyway? A tan would look good on you—and you needn't burn if you're careful."

David tried to smile, but it felt forced. He'd just begun to get to know Allen. Now he might never see him again.

Allen chucked him lightly under the chin. "Don't look so sad, kid. It'll be fine." He picked up his gear and backed slowly away. "Just remember one thing—you're not alone."

Allen had said his car was parked at the other end of the beach from David's. David stood watching as he strode away, and waved in response to Allen's wave before the man disappeared behind a grove of trees.

As he headed up the dirt track toward his own car, David felt a strange and welcome exhilaration. Instead of the emptiness he'd expected following Allen's departure, he had a sense of fulfillment, of profound satisfaction. "You're not alone," Allen had said. And—maybe for the first time—he didn't feel alone.

Unable to repress his joy, he broke into a combination of hopping and skipping, and laughed at his own silliness. He was still skipping when he passed the concession stand. Several of the customers turned to stare, and one little girl asked, "What's that boy doing, Mama?"

David didn't mind. He just grinned and waved at the girl, and kept on skipping down the road.

JAMES CROSS GIBLIN

The events in this story never happened to me. But I *was* a teenager in the early 1950s, living in a small northeastern Ohio town near Lake Erie and struggling with the fierce emotions of adolescence.

Although readers know me today for my nonfiction books, I began my writing career as a playwright. My first published work was a one-act play, *My Bus Is Always Late*, and a dramatization I made of William Styron's novel *Lie Down in Darkness* was optioned for Broadway production in the late 1950s but not staged.

After building a reputation as a children's-book editor in the 1960s and 1970s, I started to write for children myself. A number of my books have received awards and honors. *Chimney Sweeps: Yesterday and Today* won both the American Book Award for juvenile nonfiction and the Golden Kite Award for Nonfiction. Two other titles, *Walls: Defenses Throughout History* and *Let There Be Light: A Book About Windows*, were also named Golden Kite winners. Nine of my books— most recently *The Riddle of the Rosetta Stone* and *The Truth About Unicorns*—have been cited as Notable Children's Books by the American Library Association.

I retired as editor-in-chief and publisher of Clarion Books in 1989, but continue to serve as contributing editor at Clarion. Among the writers I work with are C. S. Adler and Marion Dane Bauer.

PARENTS' NIGHT

NIGHT

by Nancy Garden

With thanks and cheers to the
schools that have gay-straight-bisexual
support groups, and in hopes that all
schools will soon have them.

*T*his *year my dad* didn't give me a rose on my birthday.

When I was born, he sent Mom yellow sweetheart roses and had the florist put one in a separate vase for me. Every year after that he gave me yellow sweetheart roses on my birthday, and when my sister, Josie, was born, he did the same for her, only with carnations. He kept on with my rose, too, even though by then I'd begun refusing to wear the frilly pink dresses he liked, with spotless white tights and old-fashioned pink hair ribbons.

"Hair ribbons!" my girlfriend Roxy shrieked when I told her. "Oh, God, hair ribbons!" She laughed so hard that pretty soon she got me laughing, too. Roxy's like that—happy, infectiously cheerful.

"Come on," I said, grabbing her. "Didn't you ever have to wear hair ribbons?"

"No, Karen," she said. "I didn't. I had to wear blue barrettes."

"Barrettes!" I shouted, the way she'd said "hair ribbons." I started to laugh, but then she kissed me and for a long time we didn't talk anymore.

That was in September, when we'd just come back from a summer vacation away from each other. We were drunk with love, high with it—we still are, but it was extra special at first, when we weren't worried about anyone, especially my dad, finding out. School? Ours isn't perfect, but there's this group there called the Gay-Straight-Bisexual Alliance, which we'd both joined only a few months after Roxy'd come to our school that January.

One day in March, when I still hadn't figured out I was gay, my friend Ab—Abner—and I were talking about a dance everyone was going to. "The last thing I want to do is prance around with some stupid boy and pretend I like him," I said, and Ab said, "You really do like girls better than boys, don't you, Karen?" It hit me then that I always had, and that I wouldn't mind at all dancing with a girl. Ab remarked, very softly, "We're two of a kind, then; I like boys better than girls. You know. That way. Sexually. To be in love with."

Right away a picture of Roxy jumped into my mind, with her wavy red-gold hair and deep, sea-green eyes and her wonderfully gentle hands. As soon as that happened, I said, "Oh, wow!"

Ab looked at me with a sort of sideways grin he has. "I'm gay, Karen," he said. "And I'm in that new group, the Gay-Straight-Bisexual Alliance. It's pretty good. Maybe you should come to a meeting. A bunch of us are going to the dance.

We're probably going to dance with each other. Want to come?"

"No," I said, because I wasn't sure if Ab was right about me, but then he told me most of the kids in the group weren't sure about themselves either. I still wasn't completely convinced, but I decided to go to the dance.

Luckily, Roxy was there.

When I first saw her, I was dancing with Ab, but when I noticed she was looking my way, I muttered "See ya" to him. I danced over to this girl, Ann, who he'd introduced me to. She was in GSBA and she was more or less dancing alone; I made this big point of relating to her. No, I don't know where I got the nerve. All the time I was grinning at Ann, I was praying, "Notice, Roxy, notice; notice that I like girls." Somehow I forgot that might disgust her—dumb, right? But a couple of straight girls were dancing alone or with each other, too, and none of the straight kids seemed to notice the GSBA kids much. (Well, one guy yelled "Faggot" a couple of times, but a teacher threw him out.) I didn't think Roxy really saw me.

But a little later when I was getting a Coke, she came up to me.

I got all sweaty when I saw her heading for me, and I knew I wasn't going to be able to think of a thing to say. But she just smiled and said, "You look great dancing. Is it really true no one minds if girls dance with girls at this school?"

"Well, I—I . . ." I stammered—eloquent, right? "Sometimes. I mean I don't really know. This is the first dance I've been to here. But it looks like no one minds, doesn't it?"

Roxy laughed her infectious laugh. "Yes," she said, and she actually took my hand. "It does look like that. I don't see any boys dancing together, though. I'm glad we're not boys, aren't you?"

I gulped and said, "Yeah," and we danced. We went on dancing together the whole night, and I almost didn't notice when Ab sailed by and mouthed "Lucky" at me.

Well, that's how I got to know Roxy. We had one lunch period a week at the same time, and we had a couple of classes down the hall from each other, and of course there was after school. We both went out for the same sports, not because we both liked the same ones but so we could be together. We left notes in each other's lockers. And pretty soon we were so close, we almost breathed the same breath. I knew what she was going to say before she said it, and she knew what I was thinking. We didn't always agree, so we argued a lot, but we always ended up laughing and then learning from each other—we still do. We both joined GSBA and pretty soon the other kids there began calling us "The Lovebirds." Without really saying anything about it, suddenly we, plus Ab, were the only kids in the group who were sure enough we were gay to be out.

Out in the group, that is. Not out to teachers or kids outside GSBA, as Ab was, not out to straight friends, not out to siblings, and especially not out to parents.

In September, after school started again, Dad kept saying I should make other friends, and Mom kept asking me about boys.

132

Finally Mac, who's the faculty adviser to GSBA, said, "Karen, your parents aren't going to get off your case unless you explain things to them."

I'd been complaining about how hard it was for me to pretend to my parents that Roxy and I were just ordinary best friends. I'd told them Ab was my boyfriend, and Mom had been urging me to get him to fix Roxy up with someone so we could go out together as two couples instead of as a threesome, which is what we usually did. "It isn't fair to Roxy, dear," Mom said. "Think how you'd feel if she had a boyfriend and you didn't." Mom's a social worker, and she prides herself on understanding what goes on inside people. "Don't you want Roxy to have a boyfriend?" she asked. "Doesn't Roxy want one?"

I wanted to scream "NO!" but I had to say "Yes" to both questions. I muttered something about Roxy's being shy, and Mom said we'd have to help her get over that and how about giving a nice little party.

"She's a social worker, Karen," Mac said when I told the group. "She must know something about homosexuality."

Roxy reached for my hand. "Knowing and accepting aren't the same thing. You should see her, Mac! She spends two hours a week at the beauty parlor, and she buys all her clothes at Lord & Taylor, and when she meets a woman friend, she sticks her cheek against her friend's and her butt out behind—God forbid she should touch another woman's body—and she and the other woman kiss the air."

"I love it!" Ab chortled. He grabbed the hand of a guy

133

named Jonathan who sat next to him, and they stood up and demonstrated, perfectly.

Everyone laughed, and we went on to something else, but at the end of the meeting Mac said, "I have an announcement," and we all got serious again, because Mac's rarely that formal. He's the only teacher in the whole school who's out, which must take incredible guts, and he started GSBA, so to us he's pretty much of a hero. He was usually so upbeat that the solemn face he put on then made me afraid he was going to tell us he was HIV positive or something. But all he said was "Okay, gang. You probably know Parents' Night is coming up. . . ."

We all groaned, which is the usual thing kids in our school do when someone mentions Parents' Night—"Show Time," Ab calls it. It's bad enough to have to clear out the desks and lockers, and make sure there's evidence of Exciting Meaningful Projects in the classrooms, and only great-looking artwork on the walls—but there are also parent-teacher conferences, and some kids have to serve as guides and escort the parents around the school.

Mac held up his hand. "I know, I know," he said sympathetically. "But the gimmick this year is that the gym's going to be set up with booths for all the student organizations and clubs, and I thought we should have one, too."

There was a stunned silence. Nobody said anything for a while, but finally Ann, the girl I'd danced with when I was trying to get Roxy's attention, said, "What's supposed to be in the booths?"

"A couple of members of the organization, and something to show what the organization does," Mac answered. "The drama club will have programs of past shows—that kind of thing."

"We could put out those book lists you've been giving us," said Roxy.

"And the list of gay organizations in the city," said Ann.

"And AIDS stuff," Ab suggested.

Jonathan grinned. "Hey, we could hand out condoms!"

"Don't think that didn't occur to me," said Mac. "But I have a funny feeling that might not go over big with some of the parents. The last thing we want to do is antagonize anyone."

"But AIDS stuff is a good idea," said Roxy. "The lists, too, of course."

"Good," said Mac. "Any volunteers," he asked casually, "for sitting in the booth?"

"You," said two or three people at once.

"I'll be there," said Mac, "or nearby, but the point is for the parents to see what the *kids* are doing. I know what I'm asking," he added. "Believe me, I know."

"It should be someone who's out," the girl next to Ann said.

All eyes went to Ab, and then to Roxy and me.

"Not necessarily," said Mac. "Remember, our big point has always been that no one has to be out, or sure of their sexual orientation."

"Yeah," I pointed out, "but most kids figure we're all gay,

135

and the parents probably will, too. You know what people are like."

"Yes," Mac said. "I know."

Everyone was still looking at the three of us.

Ab shook his head. "My dad would throw me out of the house. I know he's coming to Parents' Night. I'm sorry. I'd really like to do it, but I can't."

"You mean you're not out to your folks?" asked one of the other boys. "Jeeze, you're out to everyone in this whole school!"

"I know, I know. But at home I'm a master of subterfuge." Ab gave a little bow, and we all laughed, but uncomfortably.

"That leaves us," I said to Roxy. "But we're not out to our parents either," I said to everyone else.

"No one has to make a decision now," Mac told us. "But do think about it, everyone. And remember, it really doesn't have to be anyone who's out, or anyone who's sure of their sexuality."

"But no one who's not sure is going to dare," Roxy said later, up in my room; my parents were still at work. She hesitated. "My dad's got one of his trips that week, I think, and Mom's going with him." Roxy's dad was in the travel business, and she and her older sister often had to stay alone.

"Lucky!"

"I'm not absolutely sure yet." Roxy smiled bravely. "But look, if I have to do it—be in the booth alone, I mean—it's okay. Maybe it would be better."

"I can't let you do that," I said. "God knows how people are going to react."

"Mac'll be there." She kissed me. "Don't worry."

I kissed her back, deciding quickly. "I'll be there too."

But how, I asked myself after she left, am I going to tell my folks? I knew I couldn't just suddenly appear in the booth without warning them.

I went over lots of scenes in my mind, starting with the one where I come down to dinner and say, "Mom, Dad, Josie, I've got something to tell you. I'm gay. I'm a lesbian"—whereupon Mom throws her hands up to her face and bursts into tears and Josie stares at me like I've just grown another head, and Dad shoves his chair back and says, "I'm going out"—and ending with the one where I say quietly on Sunday while we're all reading the paper, "By the way, I'm going to be in one of the student organization booths on Parents' Night," and Mom says cheerfully, "That's nice, dear. Which one?" and I say "GSBA," and Dad says, "What in blazes is that?" I say "Gay-Straight-Bisexual Alliance," and they *all* stare at me like I have two heads. Mom says, "Do you think that's wise, dear?" and at the same time Josie says, "Gay as in homosexual?" Dad bellows, "I don't want any daughter of mine mixed up with a bunch of queers. You want to do social work, you go to school for it like your mother. *Then* we'll talk about it."

But as it turned out, I didn't have to play any of the scenes I'd imagined.

Three nights later, at dinner, Mom said, "I had to turn down two more cases today. I really wish my supervisor would get it through her head that I just can't handle AIDS cases."

Now, this wasn't a new topic. Mom's okay as a social worker, I guess, but she'd developed this one serious blind spot: She'd refused to handle AIDS cases ever since her supervisor first tried to give her one, saying she was trying to protect our family's health. This had started back before I knew much about AIDS. Later, when I knew more, I made a feeble attempt at telling her she couldn't catch AIDS unless she slept with her clients or got their "body fluids" in a cut or something, but she just said, "Medical science isn't infallible; there's a lot people still don't know. I can't risk your health." At that I'd given up.

But tonight, since all I'd been thinking about was that darn booth and how sick I was of hiding from my parents anyway, I just fell apart.

I tried to be calm at first. "Who gets the AIDS cases you give up?" I asked. I could hear that my voice sounded funny, and I guess everyone else did, too, because Mom, Dad, and Josie all stopped eating and stared at me.

"Why, I don't know," said Mom. "But they do get re-assigned, eventually."

"Oh, great," I said sarcastically. "And until they do, some poor gay guy languishes in his rented room, too weak to go out and get food or cash his welfare check or whatever."

Mom and Dad looked at each other.

"Karen," Dad said to me, "your mother is a very good social worker. She is also a very good mother, and she's told you before why she won't take AIDS cases. You should be grateful."

I laughed. "Isn't that just a little bit hypocritical? I mean,"

I went on, turning to her, "if you really believe you're going to catch it, aren't you condemning some other social worker and her family to certain death by letting the cases be reassigned?"

Mom looked startled, and then I swear she turned pale. "I know the risk isn't great, Karen," she said evenly, but I could hear that she was furious. "And I believe most of the workers who accept AIDS cases don't have families. Some even volunteer. I just happen to prefer working with normal people who need social services through no fault of their own."

Then I really exploded. I could feel it coming, but there wasn't any way I could stop it. "Fault of their own!" I yelled. "Normal people! God, how unfair. What you're really saying is that if my gay brothers and sisters get AIDS, it's their fault and they deserve to get sick!"

There was a deadly silence. I mean deadly. The kind that chokes you.

"I thought it wasn't just gay people," Josie said, looking around anxiously. "They said in health class that it's drug addicts using dirty needles, and people not using condoms, and you don't have to be—to be gay, Karen. Normal people can get it, too, and kids can, and people have gotten it from bad blood transfusions, and—"

"What do you mean, your 'gay brothers and sisters'?" Dad boomed, ignoring Josie.

Suddenly I was freezing cold, and my heart was beating so hard I felt dizzy. I took a deep breath and looked Dad straight in the eye. "I mean I'm gay too," I said as calmly as I could. "I didn't want to tell you this way, yelling it, and I'm sorry I did, but I'm tired of hiding. I'm a lesbian, and Roxy and I, we're not just friends like you think, we're—"

"That's enough," my father snapped. "Josie, please go to your room."

"But Daddy—"

"Do what your father says," Mom ordered. She'd sort of moaned when I'd said the word "lesbian," and now I could see that she was fighting tears.

I got up and tried to put my arms around her, but she pulled away.

"I—I'm sorry," I said, going back to my chair. "I'm sorry. But that's how it is—how I am. I can't do anything about it; I don't want to. I never fit in before, because I didn't know where I belonged or what made me different. Now I do. And I wanted you to know. I'm in this group at school . . ."

I told them about Parents' Night and the booth and how Roxy and I were going to be working in it, but when I'd finished, my father got up from the table, looked at me coldly, and thundered, "You are not going to be in that booth. And you are going to drop out of that—that organization. If I have to take you out of that school and send you to another, I will." He stormed out of the room.

My mother let go her tears, and followed him.

I didn't drop out of GSBA, and luckily my parents didn't mention it again. Two days later was my birthday, and we had the usual family party, with cake and ice cream and presents. My parents had been pretty strained and distant, but they went ahead with all the traditional stuff almost as if nothing had happened, singing "Happy Birthday" and marching in with the presents and the blazing cake. I oohed and aahed, and there was a certain amount of false laughter. But there was no yellow sweetheart rose from Dad, and he was the most strained and the quietest of all of us. You better believe I noticed, and after dinner I went to my room and cried.

Time went on and things slowly settled down on the surface, except I noticed a list of names near the phone one day that I figured might be psychiatrists, and I almost threw it away. No one said anything about it, though, so I didn't. Then one Saturday a couple of weeks later Dad went fishing with a friend of his at some ungodly hour like five A.M. Josie slept late, so I had Mom to myself when I went down for breakfast. She said, "Good morning," cheerfully and made us both bacon and eggs, and we talked about the weather and how many fish Dad might or might not catch. But when she started on her second cup of coffee, she finally said, awkwardly, "Karen, I'm sorry about the—that argument."

"I am too," I said. "I'm sorry I attacked you. I don't agree with you about AIDS, and it's something that matters to me. But I guess you have a right to your opinion."

"Maybe I don't," she said, "if my opinion is wrong. I've been doing some reading, and I'm a little ashamed of myself. I—I think I've lost sight of why I became a social worker in the first place. I've always been—uncomfortable, I guess you could say—about homosexuality. But . . ."

"There are parents' groups," I told her tentatively.

"Yes," she said with a sort of embarrassed smile. "I know. Parents, Families and Friends of Lesbians and Gays. I've talked with a very nice woman, several times. She's helped a lot.

Karen, I—I'd rather you weren't gay. And I don't quite believe you are; you're so very young. But if you are, if you turn out to be, I want you to know I still love you, and I'll do my best to support you. I like Roxy," she added shyly. "And I'm glad you—you've got her."

"Me too," I said. Then, carefully, I asked, "Are you and Dad coming to Parents' Night?"

"I am. And I've been trying to get Dad to come, too. Are you going to do that booth?"

I took a deep breath. "Yes," I said. "With Roxy."

Her lips tightened, but she nodded and finished her coffee.

By the time Parents' Night came, though, I still didn't know if Dad was coming. He'd caught several big trout on his fishing expedition, and we'd had them for dinner that night rolled in oatmeal and fried the way he liked them. I helped Mom cook them, and he seemed pleased at that. He wasn't really hostile anymore, but I kept catching him looking at me like I was some stranger. A couple of times I wanted to say, "Hey, Dad, I'm still the same person I always was; it's just that you know me better now." But I didn't dare.

The night before Parents' Night, I had a bad case of nervousness when Roxy and I and the other kids set up our booth. Some of the straight kids looked at us kind of funny, but I guess Mac's being there kept them from saying anything. When we got back to the gym that night, though, a while before the parents were due, someone had painted "FAGGOTS AND DYKES" over the words "GAY-STRAIGHT-BISEXUAL" on our sign.

"Ignorant bastards," Mac muttered, and Ab, who'd brought the AIDS literature, said, "I'll fix that," and he ran off to the art room. By the time the doors to the gym opened and the parents started coming in, the sign said the right thing again.

"Are you as nervous as I am?" I whispered to Roxy when Ab had left.

She nodded, and Mac pretended his hands were shaking and his head and his whole body, and that made us laugh. A few minutes later the principal came up to us and said, "You folks get the prize for bravery. Good luck, and let me know if there's any problem." That was pretty nice.

There wasn't much of any problem. A few parents came up sort of hesitantly, like they were surprised or embarrassed, and that helped me feel less scared. One or two walked by grinning or giggling as if we were aliens or something, and one man stopped in front of the booth, shaking his head and saying "I don't believe this" over and over, but no one paid much attention to him. Lots of people took AIDS literature, a couple of people said they were glad we were there, and a few people took the book and organization lists.

And then I didn't see much else, because I spotted my parents coming into the gym.

Right. My *parents*. Plural. Mom was smiling bravely, and hanging on to Dad's arm as if she were trying to show the world he belonged to her and they were a happy, well-adjusted couple. Well, okay, I figured I'd do that kind of thing, too, with Roxy, if I could. Dad's left arm, the one that wasn't linked with Mom's, was behind his back. Without even glancing at any of the other booths, he led her right up to ours.

143

Talk about cold sweats!

I put as much of a smile on my face as I could and started to say, "Hi. Thanks for coming."

Dad looked very embarrassed, and as nervous as I felt. He sort of scanned the gym as if he were checking for people he knew, and he gave Mom a desperate look. She nodded in a stiff kind of way, and Dad bent down awkwardly so his head was sort of half inside the booth, and he kissed me.

Then he took his other arm from behind his back and handed me a yellow sweetheart rose.

"Happy birthday, kiddo," he whispered. "I'm a little late with this, but I promise I won't be again. I—I've got a lot to get used to, but—well, you're still my daughter. I just need some time." He smiled, a little crookedly, but hey, it was still a smile.

I couldn't move, and I felt tears well up in my eyes. While I was still trying to figure out what to say and how to keep from blubbering all over the booth, Dad reached over to Roxy and gave her shoulder a clumsy pat. "I'm glad you and Karen care for each other," he said awkwardly.

He looked around the booth and picked up the lists and some AIDS pamphlets. He handed the AIDS stuff to Mom, winked at me, and then they walked off, heading for the next booth.

And I stood there with the tears spilling over and Roxy gripping my hand till Mac gave me a handkerchief and Roxy whispered, "Hey—crying's bad for business," and we went back to work.

NANCY GARDEN

I was born in Boston, started writing at eight, and haven't stopped since, although I've had lots of other jobs.

The idea for "Parents' Night" came from a visit I made to Cambridge Rindge and Latin School in Cambridge, Massachusetts, where there's an organization called Project Ten East, modeled after a similar group in California. It's for gay and straight kids, for the purpose of providing counseling, information, friendship—whatever's needed. I'd love to see similar groups in schools all around the U.S.

I've written many books for young people, but closest to my heart is *Annie on My Mind*, a lesbian love and coming-out story, which was chosen by the American Library Association as a Best Book for 1982 and one of their Best of the Best for 1970–1983, was on the 1982 *Booklist* Top Choice list, and was nominated for a couple of awards. A radio version of *Annie* has been broadcast twice by the BBC in England. My next gay book was *Lark in the Morning*, which is not a coming-out story but is about a teenage lesbian who risks widespread disapproval by helping two runaways. I wrote *Lark* partly because I feel there should be books about gay kids in which being gay is important but not necessarily pivotal in itself—as being straight is in most other young adult books.

Right now, among other projects, I'm working on another coming-out novel, and one, dealing with AIDS, about a friendship between a young lesbian and a young gay man. A gay story of mine will appear soon in *Rooms of Our Own*, a forthcoming feminist anthology.

MICHAEL'S LITTLE SISTER

▽

by C. S. Adler

For David, my good friend
and Cape Cod neighbor

*M*ichael's ten-year-old little sister wasn't home yet when he got there after his seventh-period physics lab. That was odd, but he didn't worry about it too much. Becky was probably crouched behind some bush, totally absorbed in watching a curious insect eating or procreating or fighting for survival. Anyway, he had other things on his mind. He looked up Walt's number and dialed it fast before he lost his nerve.

"Walt? It's Michael."

"I know who it is." Walt's deep voice was so full of counterpoint that it seemed to mean more than he was saying.

"I'm calling to apologize," Michael said. He bit his lip against the tremor in his voice.

"Good. You're forgiven."

"Well, can we talk about it?"

"You're not afraid I'll contaminate you?"

"You said I was forgiven." He wasn't going to

take any grief from this guy even if he was a hotshot senior. Sure Michael had backed off, but who wouldn't? Associating with Walt meant getting labeled, and the label might not fit— probably didn't fit, Michael reassured himself.

"Right," Walt said agreeably. "When you're right, you're right. *I* apologize for the dig. . . . So okay, bring your clarinet over tonight. After the jam session, you and I can talk."

"I'd like that. I mean I really would, but my mother works the hospital switchboard nights, and I have to stay with my little sister."

"You mean you're stuck in every night?"

"Not weekends. Just school nights."

"Okay then. I'll send the guys home early and come to your house. Say around ten? Your little sister should be beddy-bye by then, right?"

"She will be." The cool note Michael had intended came out anxious and breathy. He chewed his lip and asked, "Do you know how to get to me?"

"I've known where you lived for a long time, Michael." Again the counterpoints. Michael's heart squirmed in an agony of delight. Rumors or not, Walter Turner didn't notice every lowly junior.

He had an urge to call up Wendy to ask if she thought Walt might just be interested in him because he played the clarinet, but he couldn't call Wendy, not after this weekend. Thinking of that night depressed him. For the tenth time Michael asked himself how it had happened. Wendy Carr had been his girlfriend for three years, ever since he'd helped her get her locker open the first day of high school. And Wendy had whipped-cream skin and a chuckling laugh that was infectious. Why, then, hadn't kissing her ever thrilled him as much as the unspoken meanings in Walt's voice?

Wendy had kicked him out for good Saturday night. "Forget it," she'd told him. "You don't want me, Michael. I don't turn you on." He should never have pulled back when she'd wanted him to touch her there. He should never have pulled back, even though she'd startled him and he couldn't help his reaction. No other boy would have pulled back at the sight of Wendy's naked body. No other boy who was normal, that is.

Feeling slightly nauseous, Michael went to the refrigerator for some Coke. It was Mom's stomach-ailment remedy. Before she'd gotten health-care coverage with her second job, she'd avoided taking them to the doctor, and the medicine cabinet was stuffed with home remedies she'd tried on them. Luckily, neither Becky nor he was ever very sick.

The Coke didn't help. Michael tried to remember if he'd eaten lunch. Lunch was when Walt had joined him in the sunny alcove in the courtyard outside the cafeteria, where Michael had gone to eat his sandwich alone rather than face Wendy and her friends. He was afraid she'd have told them. Maybe not, though. He hoped not.

"So," Walter had said. "I understand you're pretty good on the clarinet. A bunch of us get together to play at my house now and then. You interested?"

"I don't know," Michael had hedged. The rumor was Walt

was gay. He didn't look gay to Michael. He was tall and well built, with formidable eyebrows above sharply intelligent eyes, and he moved like a tiger on the soccer field, where he was a star. That was along with being the star in the drama club's modern version of *Hamlet* and being an honor student.

"Don't know what?" Walt asked.

"Why you're asking. I mean, is it just because I play clarinet or—?"

Walt's eyes narrowed. "I didn't ask you to go steady, Michael," he said. But then the anger faded and his lip curled in a lopsided smile as he added, "Just for a date."

"I've got a girlfriend," Michael had said. He heard his own awkwardness and hated it.

Walt's smile stayed put. "How come you're not eating lunch with her today? Isn't she treating you right?"

"We just had a fight. Anyway, there are other girls." Weak defense, Michael thought. What he should have done is tell Walt it was none of his business.

"You don't know yet, do you?" Walt had murmured in a deep, amused voice.

"Know what?"

"Who you are." A kindness softened Walt's eyes as he said, "Well, don't worry, Michael. You're not alone." Then he'd sauntered off.

Watching him go, Michael's heart had beat at breakneck speed, and he hadn't been at ease with himself since. Was he giving off some kind of scent, that Walt had zeroed in on him so soon after the fiasco with Wendy?

▼

At three Becky still wasn't home, so Michael called the neighbor whose garden was her favorite hunting ground for bugs. No answer there. Who could he call next? Last year, when she was nine, Becky had had a friend, a Korean girl who had helped her collect the moss and plants and sticks for the terrariums filled with live insects that lined the shelves Michael had built Becky for her birthday. Hee Chung had moved away at the end of the summer, and Becky had given her her prize possession, a slim turquoise-colored beetle, shiny as enamel, that she had found in a vacant lot behind the school.

"You'll make another friend," Michael had promised his little sister to chase the sadness that had wilted her for weeks.

"No. I won't. Hee Chung was the only one like me," Becky had said.

"You're not that different, Becky."

"Yes, I am. I'm different. But it's okay, Michael, because I have you." Her fern-green eyes told him without words how wonderful he was.

They had always been close. Becky had been a baby in Mom's arms when their father had been killed at the dangerous intersection on Route 7, the last one to get it there before they installed the traffic light that people had been demanding for years. After Dad died, Mom was always working and too tired to read picture books to a quiet little girl or play Candy Land with her or listen to the songs Becky learned in kindergarten. Michael had done that. He'd pasted on the Band-Aids and kissed the booboos and washed all their

153

T-shirts and socks in the ancient washing machine that kept breaking down and tearing holes in things.

At three thirty Michael called the only other place he could think of—the elementary school. The school secretary remembered Michael, and she chatted with him fondly before informing him that Becky had been sent to detention. "I'm surprised she didn't reach you, Michael. I told her to call. Were you on the phone? Anyway, she'll get out and be home soon. Don't worry, dear. She's safe."

"You wouldn't want to tell me what she got in trouble for?" Becky was so careful to obey all the rules that she never even forgot to do her homework, something Michael had been known to forget frequently.

"I'll let her tell you herself," the school secretary said. She was right, of course, Michael thought.

With Becky accounted for, he went back to thinking about himself. "You don't know who you are yet, do you?" Walt had said. Michael had always *thought* he'd known. He was the good son. Mom always said that. "I don't know how I'd manage without you, Michael. You're such a good son." He was the musical one, the kid who could play any tune by ear on a piano even though they'd never had the money to own one. The clarinet had been his combination birthday-Christmas present last year. He went for it now and fitted it together and blew softly into the mouthpiece. The music soothed him, as it always did. Once he was in the music, it didn't matter who he was. He was the maker of sounds that filled the air with a jungleful of hidden tropical birds—high notes and low, mellow as sunshine, soft as the spongy forest floor, mysterious.

Becky came in through the kitchen door, the door they were supposed to keep locked and never did. She perched on the step stool with her books in her lap and said shyly, "Hi, Michael."

He lowered the clarinet. What a wispy little thing Becky was. She was as fragile as one of her damselflies. "So how did you get in trouble?" he asked to get it over with.

"You know already?"

"I called the school to find out where you were."

She buried her face in her arms and scrunched up her knees, making her shape into a lump draped with fronds of limp brown seaweed hair.

"Come on," he said. "It can't be so bad. Everybody gets in trouble sometime or other. What happened?"

"I can't tell you."

"You hungry? I saved you two cookies."

"I'm not hungry."

"Okay," he said with a shrug. "I guess you don't trust me."

"Oh, Michael. I trust you. You know I trust you. But—"

"But just not that much, huh?"

"I punched a kid in lunch," she burst out, unable to bear his accusation.

"Why?"

She shrugged and wouldn't answer.

"Well, then, who was it?"

"Wendy's brother."

"That big ape? You punched *him*?"

155

"I had to. He called you a name, Michael."

"What name?" He was afraid he knew, but he had to hear, just the way he used to have to poke a loose tooth with his tongue. Becky didn't want to tell him. It took some coaxing to get it out of her.

"He said you were a fag."

"Oh," Michael said, and although it was what he'd suspected, the plug pulled out of his stomach.

"You're not, Michael, are you?" Becky asked.

That she needed to ask shocked Michael so much he blurted out fiercely, "Of course not."

"Good." Becky's sigh of relief was huge for such a small girl. Well, why shouldn't she believe him? He'd never lied to her. And he might not be lying now. It could still be just a mistake.

"I'd like the cookies now, I think," she said.

Mom called at six, as she usually did, to check up on them.

"Spaghetti with clam sauce again," he told her when she asked what they were having for dinner.

"Don't you two ever get tired of spaghetti?" Mom asked. "There's hamburger meat in the fridge."

"Becky likes spaghetti." It was easier to let Becky's food tastes determine what they ate, because she didn't eat at all unless what was offered appealed to her. She'd go without food for days until he feared she was starving to death. For one solid year he remembered having bananas with every meal. Then they'd gone through a cereal-and-milk phase.

Spaghetti was a step up from that.

When Mom had her days off, she cooked mostly chicken and hamburger and beans. She was a terrible cook. Even before she'd taken on the night job on the switchboard at the hospital to supplement their income from her hairdressing, she'd been a terrible cook. Michael did better. Mom claimed he did everything well. She wanted him to get great marks in school and go to Harvard and become a doctor. Michael found getting great marks tedious. He could do it; he just didn't want to give up his friends and his music and his thinking time, which is what it would take. Anyway, what he wanted was to do something with music. He didn't care what. Being a disc jockey might be fun.

"Do you have time to play a game with me tonight, Michael?" Becky asked as they washed the dishes together in companionable silence after their spaghetti supper.

He didn't have time if he was going to make notes for the report on Chinese pottery for Global Studies II before Walt came, but she had punched out Wendy's big little brother on his behalf, so he said, "Sure. Scrabble or cards?"

"Clue maybe, or Risk." Those were the games he liked. He wondered why she was trying to please him.

They played Clue, but she didn't seem to care if it was Miss Scarlet in the kitchen with the knife or Professor Plum somewhere with the gun. "What's the matter, Becky?"

She couldn't tell him, though. It had always been hard for her to tell things, even to him. "Your little shadow," friends called her for the way she hung on him and looked up to him and did what he told her without argument. But she'd never had a father. He was Becky's father-brother. Most of the time he didn't mind. He liked that Becky depended on him, and he did his best to take care of her.

Nine thirty was her usual bedtime, but tonight she kept delaying, as if she knew he wanted her out of the way for Walt. She dragged the game out, reluctant to take her shower so he could come to read her a bedtime poem from the hundred best poems book he'd bought her. After that the rest of the evening belonged to him. Usually he waited up for Mom, who liked to tell him what she'd had to put up with at work, and hear his and Becky's news of the day.

Finally at ten, when Walt was due to arrive, Michael said none too gently, "Becky, a friend of mine's coming over pretty soon. How about calling it a night, huh?"

"A girl friend?"

"No, a boy friend."

She looked at him carefully. "Do I know him?"

"No, he's a new friend. He wanted me to come to his house and play my clarinet. He's got a musical group that meets there, but I told him to come here."

"Because of me?"

He shrugged. She got the message, swallowed hard and headed off to bed. Just as she called him for the nightly reading ritual, Walt rang the bell. Michael let Walt in, then went to Becky's room to say, "Good night, little sister. I'll read you a long poem tomorrow night, okay?"

She nodded, accepting that she'd forfeited her poem through her own tardiness.

When Michael returned to the living room, Walt was rif-fling the magazines on the rack next to the big armchair where Mom liked to curl up. They were old magazines, back issues from the beauty parlor. She liked reading about the love lives of famous people and movie stars.

"Interesting reading material," Walt said.

"Yeah, sure." Michael wasn't about to put his mother down by saying the trashy publications were her taste.

"So what kind of music do you listen to?" Walt asked.

Michael went for his tape deck. He put on a jazz piece recorded from his favorite Thursday-afternoon radio program.

Walt sat down on the frayed, wine-velvet couch to listen. Michael sat in his mother's chair. "Are you afraid of me?" Walt asked when the tape had ended.

"No," Michael said. "I just don't know what you want with me."

"Friendship," Walt said. "I think you're a very appealing guy, and you're pretty confused right now."

"I don't understand how you know that," Michael said slowly.

"I've been watching you. That's always the way it is, Michael. Everybody knows before you do."

"Knows what?"

Walt just laughed and patted the cushion next to him. Michael found himself getting up and moving over to the couch even though an alarm bell was ringing in his chest. It was Walt who selected the next tape. When he came back to his place on the couch, he laid his arm across Michael's shoul-ders. Michael shivered at the touch but didn't move.

Was it true then? Michael asked himself. Becky had punched that kid in the nose for calling her brother a fag, but then she'd asked. She'd wanted to hear him deny it as if she wasn't absolutely sure. How could everybody know when he didn't know himself?

When Walter kissed him, it was the strangest sensation, like a bee buzzing over a flower, natural and summer sweet. When he'd kissed Wendy, it had been low tide and sticky. That was it then, wasn't it? He was a fag.

In the morning Mom woke him to say, "Becky won't get up. She says she's not going to school. I took her temperature, but nothing's wrong with her. You want to go talk to her, Michael? I have to get to work."

He told his mother not to worry and went off to the bathroom. What now? In the mirror he saw his same old face, an expressive face with well-defined cheekbones and a broad forehead. His eyes were good—"beautiful," girls said, liquid brown with golden highlights. "Fag," he said to himself. "Fag, gay, fairy, fruit, homo." Why should this happen to him? He shuddered and washed his face and brushed his teeth. He didn't need to shave yet. His skin was as smooth as a girl's. Suddenly he hated how smooth his skin was.

Next he had to go to Becky's room. But he didn't know what to say to her. What could he say? He had lied to her yesterday for the first time in their lives. But if he told her the truth now, she'd hate him. She would think he was a monster. It could damage her for life to find the brother-father she adored was queer.

Maybe he should tell Walter to go find himself another "friend." If he fought it, he might make it change. Call up Wendy and apologize and tell her he was crazy about her and would she go out with him again. Yeah, maybe he should try that. He could make himself be—make himself be what he was not.

"Michael?" It was Becky calling him. He found her sitting in her chair by her bedroom window, which looked out on the wall of the brown-shingled house that shouldered up to theirs. Her knees were drawn up inside her nightgown—she wore flounced flannel nightgowns year round. The insects were crawling around quietly in the old jelly and mayonnaise and spaghetti-sauce jars on her shelves. The room was dark and quiet as a cave.

"Becky, you've got to go to school."

"I can skip if I want."

"No, you can't."

"I saw you last night with that guy."

"Walter?"

"Yeah. You let him kiss you."

Michael flinched. "I'm sorry, Becky," he cried. "I'm really sorry. I wish—but I can't help it. I'm not sure yet, but maybe I might be—"

"You shouldn't have lied to me," she said.

"I didn't mean to. I wasn't sure."

She considered. Then her eyes grabbed his and held him tight. "It's okay, Michael," she said. "You can't help it if you're different. It's like me. I try to like the same things other girls like so they'll like me, but I really hate silly parties

161

and TV shows." She sighed heavily. Then she said, "I guess we're both different, you and me."

His eyes filled up and he went to her blindly and hugged her. "Becky, I love you," he said. Gratitude filled him, set him aglow, because always he had thought he was the one saving her life and now here she was saving his.

C. S. ADLER

I'm always bemused by authors who say writing is hard work. For me it's easy, something I do and have always done because I enjoy it. I like planning a new book when the hope is still fresh that this will be my best yet. I enjoy telling myself the story in my first draft. It's exciting to grapple with a seemingly insoluble problem and wake up in the morning with a miraculous solution. I even like rewriting, when the material is there on the computer screen and I only need to play with it.

Best of all I love getting out of myself to become somebody else for the space of a story. Of course, it has to be someone I like. I've never been good with villains. But slipping inside the skin of a person of a sex, age, race, religion, or ethnic background different from mine is an interesting challenge for me. Since my characters are based on real people, I usually can check on the accuracy of my understandings, as I did in this story.

Recent books include *Daddy's Climbing Tree*, published in 1993, in which an eleven-year-old girl finds the sudden death of her teddy-bear-dear father unbelievable. *Willie, the Frog Prince*, published this year, deals with a sixth-grade boy with an attention deficit who can't measure up to his father's expectations. *Riding That Horse, Whiskey*, which will be published in 1995, shows how a young girl wins her father's respect when she tames an intractable horse.

SUPPER

by Lesléa Newman

We are all sitting at the kitchen table; my father, my brother, my grandmother, and me. My grandmother looks little, like a child almost, waiting to be served. My mother stands at the stove with her back to us, spooning something onto the white china plates. Pot roast. She hands my father his plate first, of course, then my brother, then my grandmother, and last of all me.

My mother sits down with her own plate. She has very little on her plate; she is on Weight Watchers and measures everything she eats on a little white postage scale she keeps next to the toaster. I have only carrots and potatoes on my plate. I am a vegetarian, so I have rinsed the pot roast's gravy off the vegetables. Everyone is pouring themselves something to drink: my father Mott's apple juice, my brother orange soda, my mother diet Pepsi, me Perrier. Often my mother remarks, "What am I running here, a restaurant? I've never seen anything like it—everyone has to have their own private drink." Tonight, though, she simply looks at my grandmother and asks, "Ma, what do you want to drink?"

"I don't care, some soda," my grandmother answers.

My mother lifts the orange-soda bottle in front of her that my brother has just put down. My grandmother says, "What's that, orange? No, give me some diet, I'm getting too fat." My mother sighs and pours my grandmother some diet soda.

We eat in silence. I can hear forks and knives clinking against plates, ice cubes rattling in glasses, my father chewing loudly across the table from me as he sops up his gravy with a piece of Wonder bread. The refrigerator clicks on and begins to hum, and outside, through the screen door, I can hear the bells of the Good Humor truck fading down the street.

My grandmother is not eating. Instead she studies each of us in turn, as if she is trying to make up her mind. Her gaze falls upon me.

"Meryl, here, take some of mine, I don't need so much. You're too skinny, here, take a piece of meat." Her plate is up in the air hovering above mine, fork posed to scrape.

"No, Nana, I don't want any. You know I don't eat meat."

"You don't eat no meat? What's the matter, who don't eat meat? Everyone eats meat." She looks around for support of her argument, but finding none, she decides to try a different tack. *"Oy,"* she says in a gentle voice, "what my mother wouldn't have given, when I was your age, to have a piece of meat to put in my mouth, I shouldn't go hungry. Here, *bubbeleh*, take a piece of meat, it wouldn't kill you." She stabs a piece of pot roast, which waves off the end of her fork like a flag.

"No, Nana, I don't want it."

"Here, Steven," she says to my brother, who, knowing he was next, has been busily shoving food into his mouth, hoping to be excused from the table. "Take some from my plate. I can't eat all this."

"No, Nana. There's more in the pot if I want more. You eat it." My brother's voice is tired, as if he's said this a million times, which in fact he has.

"I can't eat all this," my grandmother says to no one in particular, or perhaps to God.

"Ma, it's enough already," my mother says. She has finished eating and rises to put her plate into the sink. My grandmother slowly puts a piece of carrot into her mouth. My father and my brother finish eating and leave the table; my father heading for the den to watch TV, read the newspaper, and fall asleep on the couch, and my brother grabbing his baseball cap to go outside and play stickball with his friends.

I push my food around as my mother clears the table. I feel a cool breeze of air at my back as she opens the refrigerator to put away the half-empty bottles of soda.

"Meryl, I'm going upstairs to lie down. Will you finish cleaning up?" A question I don't even bother to answer since I'm the one who cleans up every night.

I take my plate over to the sink, and as I return to gather

up the dirty napkins, my grandmother pushes her plate away. "*Oy*, I'm so full, I'm busting already," she says to me. She pushes her chair back with another *Oy*, stands up, and brings her plate over to the sink.

"I'll do the dishes, Nana, you don't have to." I take the plate from her hand.

"All right," my grandmother says with a shrug. "You want some applesauce maybe, a piece of sponge cake?"

"No, Nana, I'm not hungry. And you know I don't eat cake."

"Not hungry, she says. She don't eat enough to keep a bird alive; a piece of carrot and half a potato." I can feel my grandmother studying my back as I run the water. It takes a while for it to get hot. "What's the matter with you, you don't eat no meat, you don't eat no cake . . ." She pauses, trying to figure me out. "Meryl darling, the boys ain't gonna like you if you get too skinny. Believe me, I know."

I turn to see her smiling and wagging her finger at me, the nail shiny and red. I blush in spite of myself, but not for the reason she thinks.

My grandmother thinks I have a boyfriend, but I don't. I don't even like boys. I don't know why. Maybe it's the same reason I don't like meat and I don't like cake. I told my best friend Patty about it. I told her right after I'd gone for a walk in the park with this guy Mark, from my social studies class. He kissed me over by the handball courts, and I thought I'd lose my lunch for sure.

Patty said we should practice—maybe I would like it better.

We were up in my room studying, or pretending to study really, with our books scattered all over my bed just in case my mother walked in, which wasn't likely because she was downstairs in the kitchen playing mah-jongg with her friends, and nothing, I repeat nothing, interrupts my mother's mah-jongg games. Patty pushed aside our books and told me to lie down on the bed. "This is what Bruce does," she said, and then she climbed on top of me and put one of her legs between mine. Bruce is Patty's boyfriend and he's a senior, so I guess he knows what he's doing.

Then she kissed me. Her mouth was really soft, not like Mark's at all. She showed me what you do with your lips and your tongue and even your teeth. I started feeling funny between my legs, where her thigh was pressing, like I was going to pee in my pants.

"Then if you really like the guy, you can let him touch your boobs," she said. "Want me to show you?"

"Sure."

She lifted up my shirt and pulled my bra down, so my breast popped out of the cup. Then she put her mouth down on my right nipple, like a baby. "You stroke my hair," she said, so I did. It felt nice. I felt all warm and soft inside and I peed in my pants for sure, but I didn't care. Patty showed me on my other breast too, and then we stopped. She said after I go out with Mark again, if I still don't like kissing him we can practice some more. I didn't tell her that I'm never going out with Mark again. Maybe we can practice some more anyway. I just don't like boys. But I would never tell Patty that. And I definitely would never tell my grandmother that. She already thinks there's something wrong with me, and maybe there is.

I put my hand under the faucet. The water, like my face, is finally hot. "Why don't you go inside and watch TV with Daddy?" I say to my grandmother, who is still watching me.

"All right," she says again with a shrug. "I'm an old lady. What do I know? Nothing." She shuffles into the den, and as soon as I hear her footsteps fade down the hallway, I run the water full blast and pick up her plate. But instead of scraping the pot roast into the brown paper bag from Waldbaum's we use for garbage, I pick up the pieces of meat and put them into my mouth, one by one by one.

LESLÉA NEWMAN

Like Meryl, the protagonist in "Supper," I grew up in a traditional Jewish household. It was expected that I would grow
up, get married, and raise a family. Much of my writing
explores the conflicts and joys of being a lesbian and a Jew.
The two identities have much in common: Being a lesbian and
a Jew automatically places one inside two vital, active communities that value the group as much as the individual. Both
communities have a strong need and desire to put an end to
all social oppression; and both communities have a strong
sense of history. Sometimes being a Jew and being a lesbian
feels like being torn in two, however, especially as one strug-
gles to live in harmony among one's family of origin and one's
chosen family. This is the conflict Meryl faces as she cleans up
the supper dishes and interacts with her grandmother.

I have sixteen books for adults and children to my credit.
My titles for young readers include a novel, *Fat Chance/Slim
Chance*, and the children's books *Heather Has Two Mommies* and
Gloria Goes to Gay Pride, both of which were Lambda Literary
Awards finalists. My titles for adults include the novel *In Every
Laugh a Tear*; the short-story collection *A Letter to Harvey Milk*;
and the nonfiction book *Writing from the Heart: Inspiration and
Exercises for Women Who Want to Write*. My literary awards
include Second Place Finalist, Raymond Carver Short Story
Competition (1987); Massachusetts Artists Fellowship in
Poetry (1989); and *Highlights for Children* Fiction Writing
Award (1992). I have two picture books forthcoming:
Remember That and *Too Far Away to Touch, Close Enough to See*.

HOLDING

by *Lois Lowry*

Would *you* come and be with me, Willie? Just for a few days?" my father asked me on the phone. He hadn't called me Willie since I was maybe four. And his voice was breathless, panicky, as if the air in his New York apartment had disappeared suddenly: the kind of voice you hear on 911, when people call gasping and sobbing to report that the fire has almost reached their room, or the rapist with the knife is now at the open window.

"I'll be there, Dad. I think I can get there by tomorrow afternoon. Don't worry about meeting me. I'll take a cab from the airport."

"I know you have school, Willie. I know it's diffi—"

"Dad. It's all right. I *want* to come. And Mom wants me to. You'll be okay till I get there, won't you? Do you have anybody with you?"

"Yes." His voice was a little steadier. "I'll be

fine. I *am* fine. There are friends here. Stuart and Amanda—they're here. You remember Stuart and Amanda? You met them last summer."

"I remember. Amanda was the one with a whole lot of hair."

He laughed slightly. "Yeah. She's the one with the hair."

"Wasn't she an actress?"

"Well," Dad said, "an unsuccessful one." He lowered his voice. "I should shut up, or she'll hear me. Anyway, they're here. They got here last night. And other people are coming and going. Tricia's here now. You met her, too. Remember: the magazine editor? In the apartment next door? She's in the kitchen right now, making coffee. She said to tell you hi."

"Yeah. Hi back."

"Anyway, a lot of people have been in and out. God, Willie, an aneurysm—wouldn't Chris laugh, to die of something that nobody can even *spell*?" Dad laughed, briefly. Bitterly. Then he gasped again, went breathless again, and I waited while he fought with tears. Finally he took a deep breath and said, "Everybody loved Chris so much."

"I did too, Dad," I told him before I said good-bye and went to pack.

I called Jon, my best friend since we bashed each other over the head with blocks in nursery school. "I'm not going to be in school for a few days," I told him. "Tell Monaghan to give me an incomplete for now on the history test, okay? And I'll make it up when I get back."

"Sure. You sick?"

"No. I'm flying to New York in the morning. To my dad's. Chris died yesterday."

"Jesus. Your dad's wife died? *Bummer.*"

"They weren't married," I reminded Jon, continuing the lie I'd been living with so long that it came easily. "They only lived together."

"Yeah, like for about a hundred years."

"Eight, actually. Almost nine."

"Same thing. So listen, would you tell your dad for me—I know he probably doesn't remember me or anything—but tell him I'm really sorry?"

"He remembers you. I'll tell him. He'll appreciate it."

"Jesus. I *hate* that, when people die. Or when people's wives die. Even if I never met them," Jon said gloomily, before he hung up.

I threw a few final things into the suitcase my mom had pulled down from the hall-closet shelf. Shorts and running shoes, in case I got a chance to be outdoors, in case Dad didn't need me with him every minute. A gray V-neck sweater I'd never worn; some relative gave it to me last Christmas. A framed photograph of Laura that I could show Dad; he was always interested in hearing about my girlfriends. Then I rummaged around, found a not-too-shabby-looking necktie, blue and green paisley, and smoothed it out on top of the clothes so that maybe the suitcase lid would keep it pressed flat. I figured I'd need a tie for the memorial service.

▼

Turned out it wouldn't have mattered. People wore everything from jeans to pinstripes. Amanda, the actress with the hair (and with Stuart, the stockbroker husband), wore something that looked like a paratrooper's uniform, but it probably cost a thousand bucks. And I saw a guy wearing suspenders over a T-shirt.

I wore the tie, because it looked okay, and because my dad liked it, and he said that Chris would have liked it, that Chris had always thought blue and green was a great combination of colors.

"Chris always said some football team ought to have blue and green for their official colors," Dad said. "Chris chose the wallpaper in the guest bathroom," he pointed out. "Blue and green."

Chris did this. Chris did that. Said this. Said that. People milled around the apartment, after the service, talking about Chris, remembering Chris, keeping Chris alive for a few more hours. Then finally they gradually stopped chatting, stopped patting Dad's back, stopped sipping coffee, and they stopped cleaning up the kitchen, and then they didn't have anything left to talk about, so they went home and then Chris was really dead and Dad and I were alone.

I stood there in the blue-and-green guest bathroom and unknotted my blue-and-green tie in front of the mirror while my father watched from the doorway.

"I'm glad you got your mother's blond hair," he said. He ran one hand through his own, or what was left of it. Dad's hair was dark, and he was getting bald.

I made some sort of aw-shucks remark, which is what I do

if anyone says anything about the way I look.

"No, really," Dad said. "You're a handsome boy, Will. Doesn't your girl—what's her name? Laura? Doesn't she ever tell you that?"

Gee whiz, shrug, golly, blush, shuffle. Yeah, Dad, she tells me that.

He grinned. "Of course I've always been partial to blond, myself, as you know."

Chris was blond, like my mother.

I worked the tie loose and yanked it through the buttoned-down collar of my shirt. "I've noticed that, Dad," I said, laughing a little, keeping it casual.

"Chris thinks so, too. That you're good-looking," he commented.

I would have let it pass. But he tried to correct himself: "*Thought,* I mean. Chris *thought*, is what I meant, Willie; I just automatically said it the other way; I haven't gotten used to it yet; oh, shit, Willie, I don't think I can—"

Then his face fell apart, and he slumped in the doorway, one hand grabbing at the woodwork like a failed mountain climber suddenly clutching in desperation at the last rock between earth and empty air. He made horrible harsh, choking sounds.

I held him for a while. We were the same height now, me and my dad, for the first time. When I was little, he used to measure me and mark the place on the wall of the garage. Age two, age three, age four, and five: all in pencil, in his orderly architect's printing, so neat that it always made Mom laugh.

Nothing after age five. Dad left us when I was five.

When I was fourteen, I was as tall as my mother. But that was three years ago. It took me three more years to catch up with Dad.

Finally I steered him to the living room. I shoved the cushions from the corner of the couch where some well-meaning friend had arranged them in a bright-colored pile, and we sat huddled there together and held each other. I rocked him back and forth while he cried; and eventually he was quieter, just shuddering now and then while he caught his breath. I remembered something, suddenly. I remembered that my mother had held me in the same way, had rocked me just like this, stroking my back, while I sobbed and howled until finally there was nothing left but the shudders of rage and grief and fear that were the same that I felt from him now. My mother had done that for me when I was five and had lost the person I most loved. So I understood how to do it for him, now.

Later we changed our clothes and went out running. Five miles at a good clip, and then we shared a pizza: loaded, no anchovies. My dad loves anchovies, but he laughed and said he'd make the sacrifice for me, just this once.

"I hate that, when people act like martyrs over anchovies," I told him.

"I hate that, when people talk with beer foam on their upper lips," he told me back.

I stayed four days. We didn't do much: ran a few miles each day; rented movies each night; talked a lot. Friends stopped by in the evenings. I offered to help him clean stuff out, maybe give Chris's clothes away, but he said he wasn't ready for that.

We sorted out old photographs, some going back to when I was a rug rat with three chins. Mom was in the old ones, holding me on her lap, then holding me by the hand. Then she wasn't there anymore. Dad was with Chris then in the snapshots, and I had disappeared, reappearing only during summer visits: skinny legs, baggy shorts, Band-Aids, big ears, bad haircuts. Chris was always taking me off to spruce me up, but it never seemed to work; the new shoes got scuffed and the new shorts got torn. It was all there in the photographs: me and Chris sometimes, and Dad's shadow falling into the front of the picture from where he stood with the camera; or me and Dad, grinning and squinting into the sun, and Chris's shadow sneaking into the foreground. Some were of Dad and Chris, their arms around each other, making faces toward me, and there was my skinny, shrimpy shadow reaching across the sidewalk almost to their feet.

By the third day Dad didn't cry anymore when he looked at the photographs, and he stopped getting choked up when we ate things that Chris had especially loved, like rum raisin ice cream.

And so I went home. I told my mom that Dad would be okay, that he'd be going back to work next week, that I had promised to call him each Sunday night. My mother still cares about Dad.

And she had liked Chris a lot, which surprised me when I was a little kid and surprises me still.

I went back to school on Friday and did the stuff you do when you've been gone for a few days. I collected makeup work, made promises to teachers about reading the missed chapters, scheduled retake quizzes, and collected foul-smelling forgotten socks from my gym locker.

"I could break up a whole riot just by tossing these into the middle of the mob," I told Jon, holding the ripe rolled-up socks out in front of me. "Better than Mace. Better than tear gas."

Jon sank into a cowering crouch and did his beaten-down-slave imitation. "No, boss!" he whimpered. "Not the sock torture! Anything but the sock torture!"

I tossed the socks into a trash container in the corner of the locker room, saving my mother from a potentially traumatic laundry experience.

"Where were you all week, Will?" someone called from the doorway. "You missed the swimming meet."

"I had to go to New York," I called back.

"His father's wife died," Jon explained on my behalf, but whoever it was who had asked had already left. The door banged shut behind him. "Thank you for your inquiry and your concern," Jon said with exaggerated courtesy to the closed door. "Sensitive asshole," he added cheerfully.

The lie was back, and I couldn't live with it anymore because it killed Chris a second time; it killed him in a way that wouldn't make him laugh the way an unspellable word like aneurysm would. "Chris wasn't my father's wife," I said, shoving wrinkled gym clothes into my bag.

Jon shrugged. "Whatever," he said. "*Significant other*, then."

I ended the lie, then, and gave a tiny sliver of life back to

Chris and to my father and to myself. "Chris was a guy."

"Yeah, right," Jon said.

"I mean it," I told him. My voice had a brittle, angry edge to it. "Thank you for your sensitive concern, asshole."

"You mean *what?*" Jon asked, looking up from the towel he was folding .

"Chris was a guy."

"You mean, not your father's—" Jon looked confused.

"My father's *significant other*, as you put it, was a guy," I said very clearly, looking at him.

"All these years? What's it been, like eight or nine years? Since we were little kids? It's always been a guy? But you said—"

I gave him what I thought was a disdainful, condescending look. I did my John Gielgud accent. "I said nothing, my good man. You made certain assumptions. I allowed you to do so. It suited my purposes."

He went into his part of the act that we always did together: two British guys meeting on the street, looking down their noses at each other. Curling their lips. "I see," he said. "I despise when that occurs, when people allow other people to make faulty assumptions."

"Quite so," I replied. "Terribly tasteless of me."

"Indeed," Jon said.

We dropped the act. We could have dropped the whole thing right there, I suppose.

But I started to cry. I hadn't cried the whole time, at Dad's. Not at the service. Not back at the apartment, when everybody talked about Chris and the crazy things he liked to do. Like how once he had a couple of frequent-flier tickets and so he planned a surprise weekend trip for him and Dad, and they went to Omaha. Where other people would have gone to San Francisco or Las Vegas or New Orleans—but Chris picked frigging *Omaha* off a map, and they went, and had a great time.

And once he took tap-dancing lessons. The guy was a *lawyer*, for God's sake, and he took tap-dancing lessons, and bought cornball pointy shoes, and tippy-tapped around the apartment like Tommy Tune, just for the hell of it. My dad loved it. So did I.

"He was a great guy," I sobbed, sitting there on that crummy wooden bench in a locker room that smelled of sweat and mildew and fungus and hormones. A radiator was hissing in the corner.

Jon watched me for a minute. Then he set down his stuff and shoved his locker door closed, and he came and sat beside me. After a while he put his arm around me. "It's okay," he said, and he held on to me real tight. "It's okay."

We stayed together there for a long time, and it was like the way I had held my father until his tears ended.

Finally I could talk again, and I pulled away from him. "Penalty for holding," I announced, doing my Superbowl-referee-into-the-mike routine, with the odd little smirky smile at the end of it.

"For holding out," Jon said.

I shrugged. "Holding on," I told him. "God, you smell like

you overdosed on Right Guard."

Jon stood up. "I hate that," he said, "when someone inter-rupts a male bonding session for an armpit evaluation."

I laughed and punched him gently and collected my stuff. Then I went home to continue my life, which had changed a little, as lives do every day, inching by microspecks forward toward whatever surprises are coming next.

LOIS LOWRY

I was born in Honolulu in 1937, lived in New York and Pennsylvania throughout World War II, and went through junior high in Tokyo, high school in New York, and college in Rhode Island. Marriage took me to California, Florida, Connecticut, South Carolina, Massachusetts, and Maine. Finally, divorce deposited me in Boston, where I've lived since 1979.

I lead a very quiet kind of life. I live in the city during the week and in the country on weekends. I love books and flowers and dogs and movies and music. I live with a man who has a gray beard and a sense of humor and whose hero is Harry Truman.

My four children, two sons and two daughters, are grown. All four have blue eyes and Rh-negative blood; all four are smart; and all four are funny. But those are really the only ways in which they are alike. Two have curly hair and two have straight hair (and one, briefly, had a shaved head). Three are, as I write this, married, one has been married twice, and one has never been married. One is, as I write this, a Republican. One is a Marxist. Two have children; one hopes to be a parent someday in the future, and another never wants to at all. One is physically disabled, two are athletes, and one is something of a couch potato.

I value individuals and their differences. My newest book, *The Giver* (which won the 1994 Newbery Award), reflects that.

BLOOD SISTER

by Jane Yolen

To Jimmy and Arnold, fallen stars
The skies are dimmer without your light.

The Myth:

Then Great Alta reached into the crevice of night and pulled up two light sisters with her left hand. She reached in again and pulled up two dark sisters with her right. The one pair, light and dark, she set facing one another, belly to belly and breast to breast. The other pair she set back against back so that their hairs intertwined but they knew one another not.

"Ye are all my daughters," quoth Great Alta, "whether you look toward or away, whether you look far or near. You will not lose my love wherever your gaze should fall."

She touched their eyes with her right forefinger, their mouths with her left forefinger, and their hearts with her open palm, and thus were they made fully awake.

The Parable:

As told by Mother Anda, great-great-grandaughter of Magna, last of the Sisters Arundale:

Once there was a garden in which our mothers and fathers lived. It was a comfortable place where fruit grew without cultivation and water ran over twenty-one stones to become pure.

But one of the fathers turned to his companions and said, "I want to see the world outside the garden. Who would go with me?"

Some of the fathers said yes. Some of the mothers, too.

But there were two mothers who did not go. "We are happy here," they said. "Where the sun shines on us and the wind cools us and the fruit grows without cultivation." And so they stayed in the garden and raised their children.

Only once in a lifetime, some of the children followed the others into the outside world we call the Dales.

The Story:

Selna had never wanted a child to care for. Not a baby sister nor a little cousin. And so she had paid little heed to the Hame's infirmarer during lessons about how children were got and how they were not. Of course she paid as little attention to the kitchener's explanations about food. All Selna had ever wanted, even before she had to choose in the great ceremony before Mother, was to be in the woods with Marda.

Her voice had never wavered when she and her seven-year

sisters had been asked "Do you, my children, choose your own way?" Marda's voice had been quiet, and Zenna's quieter still. Lolla and Senja had replied in their high, light way. But Selna's answer came strong and pure.

And when she had marched up the stairs to touch the Book of Light, her knees had not wobbled. Not even when the priestess's sour breath had touched her. Not even then.

"I am a child of seven springs," she had said. "I choose and I am chosen. The path I choose is a warrior. A huntress. A keeper of the wood."

No one, especially not Mother Alta, had been surprised.

But now things were different, had been different for months. And Selna could not exactly say what was wrong, only that things were different. And Marda gone. Marda, her best friend, who had trained all those years with her and who was her companion and blood sister—the last sworn with knives at the wrist where the blood makes a blue branching beneath the fragile shield of skin, a poultice of aloe leaves applied afterward. Marda had gone missioning.

Selna's mother had found her sobbing in the night. "She will return," her mother reminded her, kneeling by the bed. "A mission year is but one world's turning."

"Or she will not," Selna had said, too miserable to hide her tears as a warrior should. "Some stay at their mission Hame. Or go to another."

Her mother nodded. "Or she will not. After her mission year in her new Hame, she may have other, newer dreams. But her decision will be between Marda and her dark sister. It is not between Marda and you."

"But . . ." The cry was out before Selna could stop it.

"But what?"

Selna's traitor mouth would not contain the words. "But *I* was her sister. Her blood sister. There was no one closer."

Her mother's dark sister kneeling at the bedside chuckled. "Soon you will understand, child."

"I will never understand. Never. I will be a solitary. I will call no one to take Marda's place."

Selna's mother stood and her dark sister with her. "Come," the dark sister said. "She will know soon enough."

Selna looked up from her pillow. *"The heart is not a knee that can bend,"* she said. "Or did you not tell me that often enough?" Then deliberately she reached over and snuffed out the candle by her bed.

Her mother's footsteps were the only ones to go out of the room. Her mother's dark sister, without a candle's flame to guide her, was no longer there.

The Song:

Dark Sister

Come by moonshine,
Come by night,
Come by flickering
Candlelight,

Come by star rise,
Come by shine,

Come by hearthlight,
Come be mine.

In the darkness
Be my spark,
In the nighttime
Be my mark.

Come by star rise,
Come by shine,
Come by hearthlight,
Come be mine.

Come by full moon,
Come by half,
Come with tears,
Come with a laugh.

Come by star rise,
Come by shine,
Come by hearthlight,
Come be mine.

The Story:

Zenna called her own dark sister the next moon. Lolla and Senja, twins in everything, called theirs together.

"It is a wonder they did not call up just one," their mother said. But she said it laughing.

Everyone joined in the laughter but Selna. Selna laughed very little these days. No—Selna did not laugh at all. She left the table where the conversation continued and went out into the courtyard of the Hame. She got her throwing knife from the cupboard and fitted it into her belt, then took down her bow from its slot against the wall. The quiver she filled with seven arrows and slung over her shoulder. Then she went out the gate.

She ran down the path easily, her mocs making little sound against the pebbles. She used wolf breath to give her the ability to run many miles. It was not that far till she would reach the woods. As she ran, she thought about how she and Marda had raced almost every day along this same path, the one keeping breath with the other. How they ran left foot with left, right foot with right. How they matched in everything— the color of their hair the same wheat gold, their eyes both the slate blue of the rocks by the little river. Only she was tall and Marda was a hand's breadth shorter.

"I love you, Marda," she had said the day they had opened their wrists and sealed their lives together.

"I love you, Selna," Marda had answered, as she smoothed the aloe onto the leaf and bound it with the vine.

They had been children of nine summers then. Now they were fourteen.

"I still love you, Marda," Selna said. But she said it to the white tree standing sentinel at the wood's first path. She said it to the three tall rocks that they had played on so often as children. And she said it to the river that rippled by, uncaring. *Twenty-one stones,* the saying went, *and water is pure.*

The History:

The women of the mountain warrior clans lived in walled villages called Hames. As far as we can tell, there were five main buildings in each Hame: the central house, in which were the sleeping and eating and cooking quarters, was the largest building. It opened onto a great courtyard where the training of warriors took place. What animals they kept—goats, fowl, possibly cows—were in one small barn. A second, even smaller barn housed the stores, part of which were kept down in a cellar, where stoneware bottles were put by with fermented drinks—berry wines and even, in a few of the Hames, a kind of ginger beer. A small round building housed a bathing pool heated by a series of pipes to a central wood heater. There were two smaller, shallower pools. From the Lowentrout essay "The Dig Arundale: Pooling Resources," *Nature and History*, Vol. 57, comes the interesting theory that one of the small pools was for the children while the other, with a separate series of exit pipes, was for women during their menses. The other building, some scholars feel, was a training center or school. Others hypothesize that this fifth building was a place of worship.

The Story:

Selna found the deer tracks by the river's edge. They were incautious tracks, scumbled tracks, for the deer was still young and looking for any kind of footing. In the imprint of one was the imposition of a large cat's track.

"Ho, my beauty," Selna said. Whether she meant the deer

or the cat was not clear.

Both deer and cat had crossed the river at the shallow turning. Selna followed them carefully, the bow already strung. She knew she might be too late. The deer might have made a dash for safety and the cat, in its frustration, got its fill of rabbit or mice. Or the cat might even now be feasting on raw venison. Or tracking behind Selna . . . but she did not believe the last. The cat's prints showed it clearly and steadily behind the deer.

She went back and forth across the river three times after those tracks and, at last, lost them both when night closed in. She was neither angry nor frustrated; only suddenly Marda's treason gnawed anew. Once Selna had nothing left to do but make a hide in a tree for sleeping, her unhappiness came over her again, wave after wave of it, like a river in flood.

Sleep would not come. Each time she closed her eyes, she saw Marda leaving.

"We will think of you," Marda had said, kissing her on both cheeks. *We.* Once, Selna knew, that would have meant Marda and Selna. Now it meant Marda and her dark sister, that black-haired, black-eyed echo, that moon child.

"I hate her!" Selna said aloud.

Below her in the woods a cat coughed in answer. Selna reached for her knife and, holding it in two hands, waited a long time for the dawn.

The History:

Here in the Museum of the Lower Dales is the only Daleite mirror archeologists have recovered, though mirrors play such an important part in Hame histories and legends. The ornate wood frame has been reliably dated at two thousand years, of a laburnum that has not been found in those parts for centuries. It was found in the dig Arundale, wrapped separately and buried some hundred meters distant from the buildings.

Many scholars have ventured informed guesses about the mirror. They include Cowan's thesis that the mirror was the property of the Hame's ruling priestess and that only she was allowed to own such a priceless treasure; Temple's more conventional opinion that the Hame, being a place of women, would naturally be filled with mirrors; and Magon's bizarre and discredited idea that the mirror was part of a ritual in which the young girls called up their twin or dark sisters from some unnamed and unknown alternate universe.

Note that all the carvings on the mirror frame are mirror images of one another, a symmetry that has been much commented upon. We do not *really* know what they stand for.

FROM *AT HAME IN THE DALES*, MUSEUM BOOKLET
PRODUCED BY MUSEUM OF THE LOWER DALES, INC.

The Story:

Dawn came before the cat. Or instead of it. Selna had finally napped a bit, just enough to take the edge off her exhaustion. The imprint of the knife handle seemed etched into her palms. Her hands ached, and her back and legs. As she climbed down the tree, her stomach rumbled as well. All night in a tree was never comfortable, but as her teacher always reminded them, *Better the cat at your heel than at your throat.* And there *had* been a cat.

She shoved the knife back into the belt and went to find something to eat. There would be berries down near the river. She had long since learned which mushrooms could be safely eaten, which could not. A good hunter never went hungry in the woods. She could always fish. When she and Marda went fishing . . .

And there it was again, the ache when she thought of Marda. It was as if she had been halved with a great sword, cleaved in two. Everything she had done before had been done *with* Marda. And now nothing ever again would be. Always and always Marda's dark sister, Callo, would be between them, whether or not there was moon or candle flame to call her out.

The ache was so real, she clutched her stomach with it, turned off the path, and thought she would vomit. Only nothing came up. Nothing.

"I am a warrior," she reminded herself. "I am a hunter." It did not stop the tears. It did not stop the pain.

The Song:

Beloved

Oh, my beloved,
My sister, my friend,
I do not know where you begin,
Where I end.

My hand is your hand,
My breast your breast,

The soft pillow
Where I take my rest.

Oh, my beloved,
My sister, my wife,
If you are severed from me,
So is my life,

So is the earth gone,
So is the sky,
So the life from me,
And so I die.

Oh, my beloved,
My sister, my friend,
You are the beginning of me
And the end.

The Story:

She fished anyway. Wanting to die and dying, she found, were two separate things. The pain in her heart could not be fixed. The pain in her gut could. She caught a splendid silvery trout with a rainbow of scales. The act of fishing made her forget Marda for a while. The act of gutting it did too. But as the fish cooked on the fire, the ache came back again, worse than before. It was so bad, she thought she might bring the fish back up again as well. But her body was stronger than that. It had taken her a day and a night and another whole day to understand that.

The body has its own logic, her mother often told her. *The heart has none.*

She buried the fish bones, scattered the remains of the fire. She had been taught well.

When she went into the woods to relieve herself, she found her pants spattered with blood and for the first time understood. The ache in her belly, the pain that spread like fire from her heart, had nothing to do with Marda after all. She was come into womanhood for the first time, here in the wood, here in her deserted state.

The body has its own logic. She laughed and said it aloud. "The body has its own logic." She covered the hole carefully with dirt, packed it down. She would have to go back to the Hame. A menstruating woman did not belong alone in a place of big cats. Especially with night coming on. She would wash in the river, and then she would go back to the Hame.

The History:

As in all warrior societies, the Amazonian women of the Dales did not concern themselves about gender. Homosexual couplings were common in the all-female society within the Hames. But in order for that society to continue, there *had* to be children. They were got in two ways. Either the women who were not exclusively female-to-female oriented went outside the community and mated with males, bringing any female offspring back to the Hame with them, or they took care of cast-off female children belonging to the outside world.

Such outside mating when done within the armies was known as Blanket Companions. A woman of the Hames who went into the nearby towns for the express purpose of conceiving a child was known as a Year Wife. One who stayed longer, but eventually returned to the Hame with her girl children, was called a Green Widow. We do not know why.

The Story:

The river was cold, especially with night closing in around her, so Selna built a fire as close to the water as she could. Then she stripped off her leathers and, without giving herself time to think, plunged into the pool.

The water scrubbed at her and she shivered at first, but soon the act of bathing made her almost warm. She looked up at the sky. The moon—full and round—was creeping over the tops of the trees.

Selna stood still and the pool waters stopped rippling. The surface was like glass. When she looked down into the water, the moon was reflected back, as clear as in Mother Alta's mirror. Selna was reflected too, as if there were two of her. Selna—and her other. Marda.

The body has its own logic, she thought, slowly raising her hands and speaking the words of the Night of Sisterhood.

She meant the words to call Marda back. If they had power—and she knew they did, everyone in the Hame knew it—then maybe here in the woods, where she and Marda had sealed their love in blood, she would come. Marda would come.

205

Dark to light,
Day to night,
Here my plea,
Thee to me.

She turned her palms toward her breast and made a slow, beckoning motion, reciting the chant over and over.

It got dark, except for the moon overhead, except for the fire crackling on the shore. A slight mist rose from the pool's mirror surface, a mist that at first Selna could see through. And then she could not.

Thee to me,
Thee to me,
Thee to me.

Her hands kept up the beckoning. *The body has its own logic.* Her mouth kept up the chant. The girls had trained so long with Mother Alta in that chant that once started, Selna could not stop. Her body was cold, almost immobilized by the cold. But the chant kept rolling from her mouth, and the mist kept rising, as if carrying away the last of her body's heat with it.

And then the mist seemed to turn and shape itself, head and hair and long neck and broad shoulders and arms that beckoned back to her and a face that was as familiar as Marda's and yet not familiar at all. And the mouth echoing her own:

Thee to me,
Thee to me,
Thee to me.

"Alta's hairs! It's cold. Do we have to stand here till dawn?"

"We?" Selna wondered if she were dreaming.

"You, Selna. Me, Marjo. Your dark sister. You *did* call me out, you know. Blood to blood. Dark to light. Only it's hideously cold. And I can't move out of this stream until you do."

"Do?" Selna echoed. And then in an instant it came clear to her. Out here, in the woods, not in the cozy warmth of Mother Alta's chambers before the mirror with the other mothers there for support, here she had called her dark sister. Marjo, not Marda. "I don't want you," she said.

"Doesn't matter," Marjo answered. "You've got me. At least for the night. Now can we go get dry. And warm?"

"Dry," Selna echoed. "Warm."

"Right," Marjo said.

It seemed so sensible, and she suddenly was shivering so uncontrollably, that Selna turned, plowed through the pool on stiffened legs, and stumbled up the embankment to the fire, which was all but out. She fed logs into it and more sticks and leaves, Marjo exactly following her movements. With two working, the fire was quickly renewed, though it took much longer for the warmth to seep through and make them both stop shaking.

The Legend:

Near the town of Selsberry is a small pond, fed by an underground stream. It is called Sisters' Pond or Sels Pond. It is said that once a year, at the Spring Solstice, when the moon is at its highest point overhead, the mist rising up looks just like a beautiful young woman. The mist woman will call you with her mist arms beckoning. "Come to me, come to me," she calls over and over. But you'd better not go. If you do, she'll drown you, just as she was, herself, drowned some hundreds of years ago when that underground stream was a great, roaring river.

At least that's what the folks in Selsberry say.

The Story:

Selna got dressed quickly and Marjo matched her, leather pants, linen shirt, leather jerkin, mocs. It was like a dance, really, the way they kept time to one another. Selna had known what to expect, of course. She had been around other women's dark sisters all her life. But expecting and *knowing*, it seems, were two very different things.

In the end Selna strapped on the belt and knife and grabbed up her bow. Marjo did the same.

"Are you really very like me?" Selna asked at last. She thought Marjo looked older, gaunter. It might have been the black hair, the darker features. It might have been the moonlight.

"Very like," Marjo said. "And not like at all."

Selna put out the fire with her moc. Together they buried the coals. There was still enough moon to keep Marjo quick and eager.

"I need to get out of the woods. I'm—"

"*We* need to get out of the woods. One moon time is bad enough. Two is an open invitation," Marjo said.

Selna hadn't thought of that. "What if a cat gets me?"

"It gets me, too." Marjo laughed, though her face hardly changed with the humor. "I guess it is true as the Book says: *Sisters can be blind.*"

"I . . . am . . . not . . . blind to this," Selna said. She found no humor in the situation.

"You do not know how to laugh. In this way we are different. And in other ways. I am you, and I am also what you will not let yourself be."

Selna turned away. "I have no wish to be what you are."

"*If your mouth turns into a knife, it will cut off your lips,* or so it is said where I come from." Marjo had turned away, too, and her voice got very quiet. "You may not wish to be what I am, but we are together. Forever."

"Forever?" Selna turned back.

"At least as long as you live."

Selna was thinking so hard about that, she did not hear the sound. The first she knew there was a cat nearby was when he had launched himself, hitting her square in the back. Without hesitating, even as she was falling, she drew her knife.

The Ballad:

Ballad of the Cat Bride

Do not go to the woods, my girl,
Red ribbands in your hair,
Do not go to the woods at night,
For Lord Catmun is there.

He'll spring upon you silently,
He'll leave you there for dead,
He'll take away your virtue
And leave you a babe instead.

He'll take away your virtue,
And he'll take away your name,
And leave you but a weanling child
To carry to your shame.

Do not go to the woods, my girl,
If you a maid would stay,
Do not go to the woods at night,
Go only in the day.

The Story:

As Selna turned, knife in her hand, she thrust upward. The cat threw back his head at the same time as if trying to fight something behind him. Then he screamed—an awful sound—and collapsed on top of Selna.

She pushed him off and stood up shakily. "What . . . ?" she began. Then she saw the knife in the cat's back and Marjo looking at her oddly.

"Lucky you drew your knife so I could draw mine," Marjo said.

"I don't know what to say,"

"That's a good start," Marjo said. "Let's skin this cat down quickly and go. It's spring. There might be a mate."

"There's sure to be one," Selna said. "But she's probably laired up with kits."

That was the last they spoke, working side by side as easily and as silently as old friends. Or new enemies.

When they were finished, another night was all but gone. They started on the path together, but the moon could find them only intermittently. Each time it disappeared, so did Marjo.

When they reached the road at last, the moon was slowly setting behind the hills. It was long gone by the time Selna got to the gates of her Hame alone.

Her mother was sleeping on Selna's bed, her cheeks still wet with tears. Selna got in beside her and put her head against her mother's back. "I am a woman now," she whispered, loud enough to be heard, quiet enough not to waken anyone.

Her mother stirred, turned in her sleep. A stray strand of white-gold hair fell across her mouth. Selna carefully picked it off and smoothed it back. "But that doesn't mean I have to forget, does it?"

Her mother woke, briefly. "Forget what, dear?" she mumbled.

"I will *never* forget her," Selna whispered. She stood and took the guttered candle from the bedside, walked out to the hearth to light it. As she bent over the fire, a voice whispered in her ear.

"I will never forget her, either."

Selna turned. And looking into her other, darker eyes, at last she smiled.

The Myth:

Then Great Alta drew aside the curtain of her hair and showed them her other face, her hidden face. It was dark where she was light. She was two and she was one. "And so ye shall be," quoth the two Altas. "So shall all my daughters be. Forever."

JANE YOLEN

I am the author of over 140 books for children, young adults, and adults. I have written in almost every genre: novels (such as *Sister Light, Sister Dark*, set in the same world as "Blood Sisters"), books of poetry, picture books, song books, nonfiction, mystery, fantasy, science fiction, horse stories, easy readers. But I am also an editor, the mother of three grown children, a songwriter, professional storyteller, book reviewer, and teacher.

"Blood Sisters" is actually a prequel to the novels *Sister Light, Sister Dark* and *White Jenna*, the two popular Nebula Award–nominated fantasy books about a mythical kingdom called The Dales where women live together in communities known as Hames. In those books as well as in this story I am looking at the many ways we tell hi*story*: through narrative, parable, balladry, folktale, and academic explanations. None is totally correct. Like the blind men with the elephant, we cobble together the truth.

HANDS

by Jonathan London

for Paul and Ken

I *was staring* out the window of the bus when he sat down beside me—the night pressed up against the glass, my own image staring back at me.

"Hey Lon, can I join you?"

"Oh, hi, Mr. Marlow. That was a great reading you gave last night!" Mr. Marlow was a friend of my high school English teacher. He was a poet, and I had finally gone to see one of his poetry readings at a coffeehouse. I was just starting to write, but I was too shy to show anybody my poems, except for one or two to my teacher, Mr. Hiller.

"Thank you, but please just call me Ray." He breathed heavily. Perhaps he had had to run for the bus. "Those prison poems . . ." he said, still trying to catch his breath. "I can't help but to . . . to cry whenever I read them. It makes for a . . . a jagged reading, I'm afraid."

He had read his poems the way he was speaking now, in short phrases with a rhythm broken by quiet gasps.

217

"It was a pretty powerful reading, Mr.—I mean Ray. You never said last night *why*, what landed you in jail. Or would you rather not—"

"I was a schoolteacher for ten years," he said, his breathing coming easier now. "English. Just like Bill. Mr. Hiller to you. In fact your teacher and I went to college together. By the way, Lon, he tells me you're a fine budding poet yourself."

"Well . . ." I blushed and turned my face toward the window. A siren wailed by, lights flashing.

"Anyway," Ray continued, "I had a habit, when speaking to my students, of touching them, of placing my hands on them, gently rubbing their backs. It's how I am. I'm affectionate by nature," he said, laying his left hand softly on my arm. I looked back at him. His eyes were striking, but kind, moist. His voice was warm. He reminded me of a self-portrait I'd seen of van Gogh—gaunt face, reddish beard, eyes intense, lost beneath heavy ridges of bone.

He was quiet a moment, gazing beyond me, into the past. Then he said, "There was this one boy in one of my classes. He had it in for me, over grades. To play on the high school football team, he needed a C or better in all his classes, but I had to give him a D—I *had* to. In a paper he was supposed to write on Walt Whitman, he wrote, 'Whitman was a faggot!'—just those four words scrawled across the page—and handed it in. Those four words burned like a brand."

A loud boom box on the shoulder of a new passenger blasted by toward the rear and didn't die until the bus driver snarled, "Cut the noise or off the bus!"

218

"Well, to make a long story short," Ray said, "he told his parents that I had 'fondled' him. His father, a big shot in the community, got the school to look into my private life. They found out I was living with a man, my lover, and they were able to build a case. It was a very conservative corner of the country, you see, and I was fired and sent to prison."

His eyes looked into mine. Red threads spoked from the dark centers. His lashes were long, and curved like a woman's.

I couldn't think of anything to say. I blinked and looked back out the window. I could see him looking at me in the window's reflection. I looked through his image, which was superimposed on mine, and watched the city jerk by. Lights and windows and doorways coming to a stop, then sweeping by, dragging little bits of me behind.

What happens behind those doors, those windows? I wondered. My mind was in confusion. I saw the shining black eyes of a boy I'd seen in a lobby at the Castro Theater. Eyes rimmed with kohl, painted lashes. A mysterious Arab girl's face on a young man's body. He wore a white turban, and white cotton swaddled his body, but it was his eyes, just one glance, that burst in my belly and sent me racing to the men's room, to reel in the lush confusion of what had just happened to me. The intense and inexplicable attraction I had felt.

The bus jerked. My mind came back to the present. Ray was close beside me. I could see in the window's reflection that he was looking away now. Silent. And I remembered last night. Ray's poems. His poems were very moving, and his body was moving, too—especially his hands. As he read, breathless, intense, his fingers played an invisible sax. They danced and fluttered to the impassioned beat of his words.

I thought about what he'd just told me. His story about his imprisonment reminded me of a short story titled "Hands" in a book my English teacher had recommended, *Winesburg, Ohio*, by Sherwood Anderson. It was about a teacher named Adolph Myers. Adolph Myers's hands would flutter about the schoolboys' heads, dipping now and again, landing on their shoulders, caressing them. Because he showed his affection, and couldn't keep his hands to himself, he was severely beaten and run out of town. A man of extreme sensitivity, who used his hands to express his tenderness—he would never again teach: He would hide his identity behind the name Wing Biddlebaum, and until his dying day his hands would flutter about him, like the wings of an imprisoned bird.

"People are cruel," I said, after our long silence. "They don't understand." I didn't know if he even knew what I was talking about, but just then the bus stopped, and he started to rise. He bent down and, swift as a bird, lightly kissed my cheek. My mouth was open, and a few of the long, curly hairs from his beard tickled my lips, prickled my tongue. People were jostling behind him in the aisle, cursing, trying to get by. He laid his hands gently on my shoulders, and his eyes gazed into mine, so darkly bright and warm, they almost seemed to speak to me—speak directly to my blood.

"Keep well, and keep on writing," he said, and then he was gone, swept along the aisle, down and off the bus.

▼

Over the next couple of months I saw Ray a few times at readings. I was always the only one there my age—seventeen—
and sometimes felt foolish, like a freak, for being there. But
Ray always had a kind word for me, and made me feel a part
of something greater than just my small world of classmates—part of a wildly diverse community of seekers and
poets, artists who with their art try to explore their deepest
feelings, and sometimes celebrate their love of life, even
amidst their fears. Unlike Wing Biddlebaum, Ray was proud
of who he was.

A few months went by. I was in the lobby of the Castro
Theater again, after seeing some fine old classic movie from
the late thirties, when I saw Ray. Or what was left of him.

"Lon!" He came toward me through the crowded lobby,
beneath the massive chandeliers from a richer era. He was
already a ghost, all lips and eyes and bones caught in a net of
veins. He reached out, and I shook his skeletal hand and in my
dis-ease could only babble, "I . . . I didn't know you were
here. How did you like the movie?" Tears rushed to my eyes,
and my voice was lost. "I can't talk right now," I said, and in
the instant we grabbed each other in a hug, holding each
other up.

Then, after what seemed an eternity, I let the stream of
people swirl me off and away. Inanely I waved, and my heart
sank. I was going to graduate soon, I was becoming a writer, a
poet, and yet I could not speak to death. At least not to the
face of death—even if it was somebody else's. Somebody for

whom I felt a great regard.

My English teacher and I went to see him at the hospital later that spring. The General was by now world renowned for the dedication of its staff in the battle against AIDS, but the place was a zoo. Too many sick and dying people, not enough staff, not enough money. Chaos and madness and the sense of blind frenzy.

But Ray's room was silent. He was hooked up by tubes to monitors and machines. He seemed to be asleep, almost peaceful. Mr. Hiller, a very big man, stood immobile like a haystack beside Ray's bed. Then he said, "Ray. We're here. It's your friends."

Ray's chest rose and fell. His hands lay outside his blanket, so white and fragile, weightless as feathers.

We waited in silence, both standing in the dim gray light. Mr. Hiller whispered something addressed to Ray; then we quietly turned and stepped out of the room.

Neither of us spoke in the elevator, my heart rising to my throat as the elevator sank. Then my teacher said, in his quiet rumble of a voice, "He'll be happy to know we were there. It's people caring about each other—that's what Ray was all about."

I was invited by Mr. Hiller to a memorial service for Ray perhaps two weeks later. A small chapel, but packed with people, including several famous poets. After the most notable of them, Allen Ginsberg, chanted "Father Death," it was my turn to climb up to the pulpit and, trembling, read a little poem I'd written for Ray, called "The Kiss":

So much unsaid, one
way or the other. That
was the first
time for me, and it
so unexpected.

And I can still taste your
beard in my mouth.
But I was pleased
when you said, "Keep well,
and keep on writing," your
hands on my shoulders, your
fiercely warm eyes on mine, loving.

I realized afterward that I had been crying, reading my small, inadequate poem in a rhythm broken by gasps. The way Ray himself used to read his poems of pain, his poems of love.

I still see my old teacher at readings sometimes. We always hug warmly when we meet, and in our eyes we hold some special knowledge, as if some great poem has been transmitted between us, borne not on the wings of words but by touch: the wings of a man, who, like a bird, struggled long against the bars of his cage, and for short moments knew the freedom of flight.

JONATHAN LONDON

I was a "Navy brat," born in Brooklyn but raised throughout the United States, including Puerto Rico. Moving every one to three years until I was fourteen, Jewish but never living among other Jews, I learned to live with a lot of confusion— about who I am, where I'm going. Though I received a master's degree in social sciences and didn't study creative writing formally, I started writing poems in my late teens. I soon started to associate with other writers and artists, and found that this was my community, these were my people. I quickly made a discovery—that many of my poet friends, and many of my favorite writers, were gay or lesbian. Just as books have always opened up new worlds to me, my new associations opened up new worlds, too. "Hands," though fiction, evolved from this period of my life.

Though I wrote poems and short stories for over twenty years—living, meanwhile, a varied life as a dancer, a laborer, a world traveler—it wasn't until I had kids of my own that I became a writer for children. Three of my picture books are Book-of-the-Month Club Main Selections: *Froggy Gets Dressed*, *The Owl Who Became The Moon*, and *Into This Night We Are Rising*. The latter book is also a Reading Rainbow selection, as is *Thirteen Moons on Turtle's Back* (coauthored by Joseph Bruchac). *Thirteen Moons* has also been named a Teachers' Choice by the International Reading Association. My new books include *Fire Race: A Karuk Coyote Tale*; *The Eyes of Gray Wolf*; and *Hip Cat*. A young adult novel, *Where's Home*, is forthcoming.

50% CHANCE
OF LIGHTNING

by Cristina Salat

I *wonder if* I'll ever have a girlfriend." Robin stamps her sneakers against the wet pavement, tired of waiting.

Malia laughs. "Is that all you think about?"

"Well, what's the point of being gay if I'm never going to *be* with anybody?" Robin shifts the big umbrella they are sharing to her other hand. Fat silver drops of rain splatter above the plastic dome. She wishes the bus would run on time for once.

"Independent women. We vowed, remember? No guy chasing," Malia says.

Robin shoots Malia a look.

"Or girl chasing," Malia adds quickly.

"You can't talk," Robin says, trying not to feel each strand of her hair as it frizzes. "You have someone."

"That's true." Malia smiles.

Robin looks at the gray, wet world through her clear umbrella. It's hat weather. Black baseball hat and hair gel. She uses both, but nothing really helps on damp days like this. "It's silly to worry how you look. Rain can make you alive if you let it!" Robin's mother used to say. She loved stormy weather almost as much as Robin didn't.

"It's Friday! How come you're so quiet?" Malia asks. "You're not obsessing about your hair, are you? It looks fine. I'd trade you in a second . . . so don't start in about my perfect Filipino hair!" She grins, reading Robin's mind.

Robin can't help smiling. They've known each other a long time.

"Guess what!" Malia changes the subject. "Tomorrow is me and Andrew's six-month anniversary. That's the longest I've ever gone out with anybody."

Robin sighs. "You guys will probably get old together." And I'll be the oldest single person on the face of the planet, she thinks gloomily.

Malia's forehead wrinkles into a slight frown. "No. I'm leaving. I can't wait to get out of here." A large electric bus lumbers to the curb and stops with a hiss. "I sent my applications out yesterday. NYU, Bryn Mawr, Hampshire, and RIT, in that order," Malia says as she boards.

They squeeze onto the heated bus between packed bodies in steaming overcoats. The bus lurches forward.

"Where did you decide?" Malia asks, grabbing onto a pole near the back.

Robin shrugs.

Malia raises one eyebrow. "It's almost Thanksgiving. You are still going to try for NYU and Hampshire with me, aren't you?"

"I guess," Robin says. "I haven't had time to decide anything yet." It's not like she hasn't been thinking about it.

College catalogs are spread across the floor of her bedroom. All she has to do is figure out where she wants to spend the next four years of her life. New York? Massachusetts? Zimbabwe? There's an endless stream of choices.

"You better make time," Malia says. "You shouldn't wait until the deadlines."

"Give me a break, okay?" Robin stares past the seated heads in front of her.

"Cranky, cranky." Malia elbows Robin's arm.

A woman wipes one hand across a steamed window for an outside view and pulls the bus cord. She vacates her seat and Malia and Robin squeeze past someone's knees to claim it. With Malia balanced on her lap, Robin turns her head toward the window and watches the city swish by. She tries to picture herself next fall, suitcases packed, excited to be going. She's almost eighteen; she should want to leave home. A new room. New city. New friends.

I can't leave, not yet! The air in the bus is thick and warm; it's hard to breathe enough in. Outside the window, sharp-edged buildings and signs fly past. Robin's head feels light and disconnected. She presses her face against the cold glass. She doesn't have to leave. She can apply to San Francisco State or USF right here in the city. Or she won't go at all. Malia's mom didn't go to college. Robin's dad didn't go either, but he wants her to. "You're smart, like your mother," he's always saying. But what if she doesn't want to go?

It's okay, Robin repeats to herself. No one can make me.

Outside the window she watches a small, mixed terrier approach the curb, sniffing the ground. Its fur is wet and matted, standing up in points. The dog steps into the stilled, waiting traffic. Robin scans the sidewalk for the dog's person. Don't they know it's dangerous to let their puppy wander into the street?

Robin stares through the window, her mind racing. Maybe it's lost. She could help. She could get off the bus and . . . A car honks loudly. Something inside her shrinks up. Malia's weight is heavy on her lap. The dog looks up and scampers back to the curb as traffic surges and the bus rumbles forward. Robin cranes her neck. She should get off, before it's too late. But she can't.

"What is it?" Malia asks, feeling Robin's shift.

Robin forces herself to lean back in the seat and breathe slowly. She's being stupid. The dog won't get run over. Its owner is probably just down the block.

They hang their jackets over the chair in Malia's small, neat room and Robin drops her baseball cap onto the desk.

"You want to see my list of goals?" Malia asks. "I read in *New Woman* if you know exactly what you want, you're more likely to get it." She hands Robin an open, spiral-bound notebook and drops next to her on the bed.

Malia Manansala

Goals for Now

Get into a good college, far away
Major in computer science or business
Get another part-time job for clothes, makeup, etc.
Have fun!

Eventually

Dressy job where I make a lot of money and get respect
Nice apartment with classy things
Old BMW or Jeep Cherokee (depending where I live)
Great friends
Marry someone loyal, sexy, and successful

"Money." Robin shakes her head. "Even if we get scholarships, we're going to be paying off college loans forever."

Malia nods. "That's why I need a big career. I'm not going to suck up to some man for money. You should make a goal list," she suggests, handing over a pen. "I need a snack."

Robin flops onto her side. Why not? At the top of a clean page, in slow, careful letters, she writes:

Goals

Figure Out Who I Am
Be Proud of Myself
Fall in Love
Do Something Good

Robin frowns at her list. How does Malia know exactly what she wants?

"Hand it over." Malia comes back into the room with a tray of hot cocoa and microwaved pork buns.

"Okay, but it's not like yours."

"Do something good?" Malia makes a face. "Can you be more specific?"

"Hey, I didn't pick on your list!"

"I don't get it. When you want to do something, you just

do it. This year you start telling everyone, 'I'm a lesbian, deal with it.' Why can't you be like that about college?"

"It's different," Robin says, thinking, I didn't tell everyone. My mother never got to know. Her mom drove a red Honda CRX with African pendants dangling from the rearview mirror. She took the highway a lot, to avoid city traffic. Route 101 South. Robin yanks her mind away.

"You are going to do more with your life than just be a lesbian, aren't you?" Malia prods.

Robin gets to her feet, shaking the damp bottoms of her baggy jeans away from her ankles. "Can I borrow something dry?"

"Come on. Seriously. What kind of job do you want?" Malia sounds like Robin's mom and dad used to—always excited about plans.

"I don't know. Something to help people," Robin says, looking through the closet.

"Peace Corps? Lawyer? Social worker?" Malia suggests.

"No," Robin says, a faded memory seeping into her mind. She used to play medicine woman when she was little, healing stuffed toy rabbits and her plastic Ujima dolls with bowls of grass-flower soup. "I always pictured myself in a funky office," she tells Malia, "where people or animals would come when they didn't feel well."

"You want to be some kind of doctor!" Malia enthuses.

Robin shakes her head. Playing medicine woman was a kid thing. "You know I can't stand blood and guts." Robin focuses her attention in the closet, taking out a black lace top and black leggings.

"How about a therapist? You could help people's minds."

"And listen to people complain all day?" Robin asks as she changes.

Malia sighs, shutting the notebook. "Well, what do you want to do tonight? I told Andrew I'd call him by four. Oh, I forgot! My mother and the jerk are going out after work. They won't be home till late. Do you want to have a party?"

"Yes!" Robin says. "Go rent some movies. I'll call for a pizza and invite everybody."

Andrew arrives first with a soggy Safeway bag tucked into his aviator jacket.

"Hey, Robbie!" he says, unpacking jumbo bottles of root beer and 7Up on the living-room table.

The doorbell rings again. Robin runs to let in Malia's friend Dan, who has brought his sister, Cybelle—a junior—and another girl. Malia has plenty of friends. Most of them are at least part Filipino.

Being a mix (African and Polish), Robin doesn't care what her friends are. She only has a few anyway, though she knows a lot of people. When her mother died at the end of sophomore year, nobody knew what to say, so they acted like nothing happened. Robin still hangs out with the same people, but just because it's something to do; not because she cares.

When Malia returns from the video store, fifteen people are sprawled on the couch and floor with paper plates of mushroom and garlic pizza.

"Party woman," Andrew teases Malia, leaning down for a kiss. "You're soaked."

"It was only drizzling when I left. Sorry I took so long. I couldn't decide!" Malia takes two video cassettes out of a plastic bag. "I got a vampire movie and *The Best of Crack-Up Comedy*."

"I love vampires!" Cybelle adjusts one of the five rhinestone studs on her left ear. "Let's get scared first."

"Go change," Andrew tells Malia. "I'll set up the movie." He nudges her toward the bedroom.

Robin watches, wondering if anyone will ever care like that about her. For some reason the wet dog she saw from the bus pops into her mind. Nobody cared enough to keep it safe.

"Hi. You're Robin Ciszek, right?" A white girl in ripped jeans and a "Save the Planet" sweatshirt sits down next to Robin on the couch. "I read your article in the school paper! I'm April, Cybelle's friend. I never thought what it feels like to be gay until I read your essay. Do you know a lot of gay people, or was the story mostly about you?" April's slate-colored eyes are wide and curious.

Robin takes a big bite of pizza. It's still hard to believe she wrote an article about being gay and submitted it to the school paper. She must have been crazy.

"I hope you don't mind me asking," April says quickly. "I'm just interested."

"The story's mostly about me," she tells April. "I don't know a lot of other gay people."

"I guess you will next year," April says. "My sister goes to UC Berkeley, and she says there's like three different gay groups on campus."

Robin feels her shoulders clench up. Is college the only thing anyone can talk about? Of course, it'll be worth it to be out of high school just to get away from the stupid notes guys are taping on her locker door: *All you need is a real man* and *Robin C. and Malia M. eat fish.*

"Personally, I'm glad I don't have to think about college for another year," April continues.

"Really? Why?" Robin asks, surprised.

April looks away, embarrassed. "It's dumb. I have this cat. I don't want to leave her."

"Guess what I brought!" Cybelle calls out as Andrew dims the living-room light. She takes a half-full bottle of brandy from her tote bag.

"I'll have a little of that," Malia says, coming back into the room in overalls and a fluffy white sweater. "To warm me up."

"Quiet—it's starting," Gary yells from the easy chair as a bold, red title flashes across the television screen.

"I want to sit on the couch," Tara giggles. "Move over, Danny."

April moves toward Robin to make room for another person. Her hip rests against Robin's. The couch armrest presses into Robin's other side.

"Oh, hold me, Andrew!" Cybelle teases Malia as eerie music fills the darkened room. Malia laughs.

April's leg relaxes against Robin's. Out of the corner of one eye, Robin looks at the girl sitting next to her. April is watching the screen. Robin's thigh sizzles.

Robin nonchalantly eases sideways until their arms and legs are touching. A faint scent of perfume tinges the air. April doesn't move away. Robin's whole left side buzzes. She sinks into the couch, holding her breath. It would be so amazing if—

If what? Just because this girl liked the article doesn't mean she's interested. Robin moves her leg away, mad at herself. On screen, a shadowy figure suddenly whirls around and grins evilly. April leans softly against Robin.

Warm drops of sweat trickle down Robin's side. The room feels dark and red. Robin could reach out, take April's hand, trace one finger over the knuckle bumps and pale, freckled skin . . .

Halfway through the vampire movie, Robin has to go to the bathroom, bad. She is tempted, but restrains herself from squeezing April's leg as she gets up.

Away from everyone, she splashes cold water on her face, smiling. Could April really be interested? I could go back and sit away from her to see if she follows me.

Feeling hot and wild, Robin unlocks the door. It doesn't budge. She pulls harder, leaning backward, and opens it a foot.

"Hi, Robin." Cybelle grins, peeking around the corner.

"What's with you? Get away from the door," Robin says.

"Okay." Cybelle runs one hand through her porcupine patch of short, black hair. "C'mere. I want to ask you something." Cybelle pulls Robin into Malia's room. She shuts the door without flicking on the light.

"Smell my breath," she says, leaning close.

A warm rush of brandy air tickles Robin's face.

"I can't go home wasted. Do I smell like pizza or alcohol?" Cybelle asks. Her lips touch the side of Robin's mouth.

"What are you doing?" Robin asks.

Cybelle nuzzles Robin's face, tracing her lips along Robin's. "Don't you like me? Kiss me back."

Robin's heart stutters. Is this for real? Cybelle slides one hand under Robin's hair and grips the back of her neck, kissing harder.

I've wanted this for so long, Robin thinks, awkwardly moving her arms around Cybelle. It's weird not being able to see. Robin touches sharp shoulder blades through the thin cotton of Cybelle's turtleneck.

I should have helped that dog. The thought scuttles into Robin's head. Why is she thinking about that now!

Cybelle sucks on Robin's lower lip. I should have gotten off the bus and helped. I could have taken it to the pound, or home. Why didn't I do something?

Cybelle's small tongue slides into Robin's mouth. Why am I doing this? I've seen Cybelle around school and never wanted to. She's got a boyfriend. She'll probably tell everyone, "I made out with the lesbian at Malia's house," for a laugh.

Robin shifts sideways. "I have to go."

"What?"

"I'm going back to the living room." Robin feels for the wall switch and flicks on the light.

Cybelle blinks. "How come? It's okay. Nobody misses us."

239

She smiles and tugs on Robin's arm, moving closer.

"I want to see the rest of the movie," Robin says, pulling away. It's a lame excuse, but what else can she say? "I want to kiss somebody I'm really into, and you're not it"?

Cybelle stops smiling and drops Robin's arm. "Oh sure," she laughs. "You're scared! Writing that story and you don't even know what to do! What a joke." She yanks open the door and walks out before Robin can respond.

Robin follows Cybelle to the living room and watches her take the small, open spot on the couch next to April. She glares at the back of Cybelle's spiked head. Who does she think she is? I don't have to make out if I don't want to!

Whirling around, Robin heads back to the bedroom and jams her feet into her sneakers.

"You okay?" Malia asks, coming in.

"Sure." Robin doesn't look up.

"Are you leaving? What's going on?"

"Nothing I want to talk about right now." Robin zips up her jacket. They walk to the front door. Robin flings it open. She can't wait to be outside.

"Call me tomorrow, okay? Hey." Malia grabs Robin's jacket.

Robin looks back over her shoulder. "What?"

"We're best buddies forever, right?"

If Malia moves to New York and Robin stays here . . . Nothing's forever.

"Sure," Robin says, looking away.

Malia smiles and reaches out for a hug. "I'm sorry you didn't have a good time. Let's go shopping tomorrow morning, just you and me. Okay?"

As soon as Robin steps away from Malia's house, she realizes she's forgotten her baseball cap. Angrily, she pops open her umbrella. It doesn't matter. There's a bus stop at the corner and she's just going home.

Water drops drum against the plastic shield above her head as cars zip by, their rubber tires splashing against wet asphalt. Robin glares at each car that passes. She will never own one. What if that dog got run over? She should have helped. A bolt of light illuminates the night. Robin looks helplessly down the empty street for a bus. She hates being out alone after dark, even when it's not very late.

Whenever someone worried, her dad used to say: "There's a fifty-fifty chance of something good happening." Robin's mother loved that saying. Her father hasn't said it much lately. It's hard to believe in good stuff when you're dealing with the other fifty percent. At least she ended the thing with Cybelle. That's something. Robin might want experience, but she's not desperate.

Thunder swells, filling the night. Robin cranes her neck, looking down the street. No bus. So it's fifty-fifty. Should she wait here, hoping no weirdos show up and bother her before the bus comes, or should she start walking in this lousy weather? Her parents used to take walks in the rain. They were nuts . . . but happy.

Robin starts to walk. A sharp wind whips by, threatening to turn her umbrella inside out. Okay, why not? She has nothing to lose. Robin clicks the umbrella shut. Rain falls cold against her face and settles onto her thick hair, expanding it. She walks fast, with the wooden umbrella handle held forward, staying near the streetlamps. Water trickles down her face and soaks into her clothing. She licks her lips. The rain tastes strangely good.

When she reaches the place where she saw the dog, Robin stops and studies the black road. A few torn paper bags. No blood or fur. It could be dead somewhere else. Or it could be off foraging in a garbage can or sleeping under a bush.

I'm sorry I didn't get off the bus to see if you needed help, she thinks. Next time I will. I hope you're safe. But maybe the dog didn't need help. Maybe it wasn't even scared. Maybe it was totally pleased to be out exploring and taking care of itself. Robin decides to picture the terrier that way.

From down the block a bus approaches, grumbling to a stop a few feet ahead. Robin hurries over. As the doors squeal open, she looks behind at the dark, empty street. She is afraid, but she doesn't want to be. Slowly, Robin turns away.

It is a long walk home under the wide, electric sky.

At the warm apartment on Guerrero Street, Robin finds her father asleep on their living-room couch. A paperback novel is spread open across his chest and his glasses are pushed up onto his forehead. Standing over him, dripping onto the brown shag rug, Robin feels tender and old. She removes his glasses and places the book on the glass coffee table, careful not to lose his page.

In her room, Robin drops her wet clothing to the floor and changes into an old set of flannel pajamas. Then she sits down at her drafting-table desk. Nothing's forever, and that's just the way it is. Moving college applications aside, she lifts two thick San Francisco phone books from the floor.

Robin thumbs through the thin A–L yellow pages slowly. There is something she can do. Something right.

Attorneys, Automobile . . . Bakers, Beauty . . . Carpets, Collectibles . . . Dentists, Divers . . . Environment . . . Florists . . . Health. Health clubs, health and diet, health maintenance, health service. A boxed ad catches Robin's eye.

Holistic Health Center
Dedicated to the well-being of body and mind
Licensed: nutritionists, massage therapists, acupuncturists
Courses in herbal healing, yoga, natural vision, Tai Chi

Medicine without blood and guts. Smiling to herself, Robin reaches for some looseleaf paper and a pen. There's a new life out there, waiting for her. She just has to find it. She moves A–L aside and flips open M–Z. By ten P.M. three looseleaf pages are filled with numbers and addresses. At the top of the first page, she writes: *Call for info*.

Robin stretches and climbs into bed with her new list. She rubs the soles of her bare feet against the chilled sheets. Maybe life is like rain. Alive if you let it be; lousy and depressing if you don't. She rolls onto her stomach. Under the information for the Shiatsu Institute, the College of Oriental Medicine, and the School for Therapeutic Massage, she writes: *Tell Malia to get April's number from Dan. Call her?!?!?!*

CRISTINA SALAT

With twenty-seven boxes shipped UPS and a duffel bag full of dreams, I moved from New York to California in 1987 to leave the 9-to-5 publishing world and become a writer.

I found a cheap room in a ramshackle house and a part-time newspaper job. The people in San Francisco were friendly, and palm trees lined clean streets. It was the perfect place to begin my first young adult novel.

Because my new house was also home to three roommates, five dogs, one cat, and one baby, the rough draft of *Living in Secret* was handwritten in the relative quiet of fast food restaurants and Golden Gate Park. The book follows the adventures of Amelia, whose lesbian mom steals her from her father's custody. Being my first book, it holds a special moment of my life.

Many part-time jobs later, I am blissfully living as a full-time writer/editor in a country home where the only noise I hear is my computer printing and the cats chasing each other. *Alias Diamond Jones* (a book about interracial friendship, featuring PBS's Ghostwriter Team) and numerous short stories, including "50% Chance of Lightning," have been written here.

The year 1994 finds me researching my mixed-race heritage along with acting, homelessness, self-defense, and powwows for the forthcoming novel *Knockouts and Dreamcatchers*.

When not working, I'm savoring the outdoors with my girlfriend or indulging in long phone conversations with old friends.

IN THE TUNNELS

by William Sleator

*I*t *was the riskiest thing* Bay had tried yet: His three-person cell—one man, two women—were going out through trapdoor 12, which was *inside* the enemy encampment.

No one had used trapdoor 12 since the enemy had made camp directly above our section of the tunnels a few days before. The enemy had no idea we were right underneath them. But we knew from the noises above us—and from what I had seen on my own scouting trips, spying on them through spider holes—that there were several helicopters and tanks up there, and many weapons, and food. Lots of food.

Okay, I know we're better off than a lot of the other tunnel fighters. We have rice that hasn't rotted yet. We have big rats that can be roasted in the smoky underground kitchen. But you get tired of eating that stuff every day, and in the tunnels there's never much to go around. And the food the enemy has! Cans of meat and soup and vegetables, and fresh bread, and delicious sweet stuff to put on the bread. I'd never tasted any of it myself, but we heard about it from messengers. No wonder the enemy are so big and fat!

But food wasn't the major objective of the mission. The commander's instructions to Bay were to wreck the tanks and helicopters, and get as much ammunition as they could carry. We have so little of our own that our only hope is to use the enemy's weapons against them. Three people probably wouldn't have time to steal any food at all. But the commander didn't want to risk sending more than one cell on this first mission into the enemy camp.

We can never fight the enemy directly. There are so many of them, and they are so much stronger than us, with all their expensive planes and tanks and bombs and guns. We're farmers. What we must do is hide, and attack them in secret. That's why we have the tunnels.

Everybody knows that Bay's cell is the toughest and most daring of all the three-person cells in our section of the tunnels. Bay was always a famous fighter, and he chose the two women carefully. Dang and Tran are sisters, whose home was burned down by the enemy. They escaped into the tunnel under their house, which led to other tunnels, and eventually to all two hundred miles of tunnels in this underground city. Losing their home made them bitter, and their hatred of the enemy is fierce. Hatred makes them relentless—and reliable.

And there's one other reason why Bay chose two women to make up his cell.

I remember the way he looked at me, two years ago, when I

was swimming with my friends in the brown river. We could spend more time outside then. Bay was already a famous fighter; the way he was looking at me was like something I had been dreaming about. No one else noticed. But I could feel what his eyes meant, and I have never been shy. When my friends had gone, I went and talked to him; I don't think he would have come to me. At first we looked at each other very steadily while we talked. But soon we were smiling. We understood each other.

Bay had been with another man before; I hadn't. But it was what I had wanted for a long time. It's suspicious for a boy and a man six years older to be friends. We knew that no one must know about us. It was not easy to find places to meet where we could be alone, and safe. Even in the jungle, someone might come quietly along. But we continued meeting in the jungle anyway. We laughed a lot when we were alone together, and cried sometimes too. We couldn't keep apart.

Of course, I couldn't be at trapdoor 12 now to say good-bye or good luck when Bay and the others climbed out of the tunnel into the enemy camp. Somebody might suspect, and I had other things to do. I was half a mile away, riding the bicycle that powers the generator that makes electricity in the underground operating room. They don't think I'm experienced enough to go on dangerous missions yet, so I do all the jobs that require stamina. I'm small for seventeen, a little over five feet, but I'm one of the strongest boys in the village. I can pump the bicycle for a long time without wearing out, even in the tunnel air. I can carry large buckets of water. And I can dig faster than almost anybody. I dug many stretches of the tunnels—and I'd been doing a lot of extra digging recently.

So I wasn't there to see them go. But I could imagine what the commander would be saying to them: the same ideas we've been taught in school, and that are written in pamphlets printed on the presses underground. "Never forget, the land is the most important thing. And the enemy came from the other side of the world to take our land away from us. But they only drive us deeper into mother earth. And we will die before we let them steal the earth."

The bicycle generator doesn't make a lot of noise. Still, most of the time I'm on the bicycle I can't hear anything from outside because the patient is screaming; there is nothing to give anyone for the pain when the doctor cuts off arms or legs. But tonight the patient had fainted. It was quiet, only the rasp of the saw and the squeak of the bicycle in the dim, flickering light. And that was why I heard the very bad omen, just before the time Bay and Dang and Tran were to go outside.

It was the helicopter from the main enemy base, miles away. The helicopter with the loudspeaker, so loud you can hear it inside the tunnels. The enemy knows that if the bodies of our dead are not buried properly, then their souls will never find peace but will wander forever. And so they play for us the wails and moans of wandering souls, speaking in our own language, crying out that if they had only given in to the enemy, they would not be doomed to wander in misery for eternity.

Of course we know it is only a broadcast, a fake, another

evil trick of the enemy. But down in the tunnels, with the dead lying curled up in the walls beside us, hearing it makes you shiver. And I did not like it that Bay and Dang and Tran would be hearing it too, just before this dangerous raid. It made it more difficult *not* to think that Bay might never come back.

The doctor also knew it was the time for their mission. "Unfortunate," he murmured, sawing carefully, not looking up from his work.

"It will only make them hate the enemy more!" I said. "It will make them more determined to succeed."

Then the doctor looked briefly up at me and nodded in approval. "That's the right attitude, boy," he said. "Soon they'll be sending you out on missions like this."

I didn't say anything; it would have sounded immodest. But I was not surprised at what the doctor said. I've always been well liked in the village. It would be different if anybody found out about Bay and me.

In spite of my words, I was more worried than ever. Why did the enemy have to broadcast the wandering souls right at this time? I pedaled harder, trying not to think of it.

But I couldn't help picturing what was going on outside. Bay pushing up carefully hidden trapdoor 12, with jungle foliage growing right out of it, so the enemy will never find it. He and Dang and Tran climbing silently out into the starlit brightness; even night outside is brighter than the tunnels. And even though this dangerous mission lay ahead of them, they would be feeling what you always feel when you leave the tunnels: the vastness of the earth and the sky, and the air that moves and does not smell of unwashed bodies and sewage. There is always that bliss when you go outside.

But they wouldn't stand around enjoying it. They would move silently from tree to tree, always alert, always keeping hidden. They wouldn't be careless, even though most of the enemy were asleep. Of course there were enemy guards. But the guards were stationed around the perimeter of the encampment, watching for intruders from outside. They had no idea that we could attack them from within their own lines. Even if the guards heard a few sounds from inside the camp, they would assume it to be their own men.

And Bay and Dang and Tran might have to make a few sounds as they entered the tanks and the helicopters. First they would plant the explosives, the most important part of the job. These were very special remote-controlled bombs, stolen from the enemy by another group. They were given to us when the enemy camped above us. Even if something went wrong after the bombs were planted, they could still be detonated from inside the tunnels. But nothing will go wrong, I said to myself, sweating on the bicycle.

And after the bombs were planted, they would take out the weapons and ammunition. They would carry it, making trip after trip, to the trapdoor, where people waiting underneath would take it inside. And then—

"Okay, boy. Enough," the doctor said. The stump of the patient's leg was bandaged. The nurse had finished cleaning up. She lit the oil lamp made from an old medicine bottle. I stopped pumping, and the electric light blinked out. And then, following the nurse's point of light in the blackness, the doctor and I carried the patient to the hospital ward. We didn't have to drag him because in the hospital the ceiling is higher than usual, high enough for me to stand upright. In most of the tunnels you have to walk bent over, or crawl.

"Go get some rest, boy. You've worked hard tonight," the doctor said after we put the patient in his hammock.

I nodded, but I didn't go to rest. I went to the false tunnel and began digging again.

The false tunnel leads nowhere. It's there to trick any enemy who might enter the tunnel complex. It goes on for a ways, curving, and then turns a sharp corner directly into a booby trap, a tripwire that will set off a hidden homemade grenade. So there's no reason for any of us to go down the curving false tunnel, and no one ever does. That made it the perfect place for my secret project. I was almost finished, and I was determined to finish it tonight.

When Bay and I had met alone in the jungle, he was very gentle with me. It was always beautiful when we were with each other. I keep thinking about how much we laughed. But we had never been able to sleep all night together. And now, in the tunnels, with no privacy at all, we hardly ever see each other alone. It's like a physical pain, missing the one you love so much. That's why I was working so hard now. It was like the way I had first just gone over and talked to Bay: When I decide on something, I do it.

The false tunnel is closer to trapdoor 12 than the hospital

is. I had just managed to attach the parachute fabric to the ceiling when I heard the commotion. It wasn't a commotion like outside; you have to be quiet in the tunnels. But you learn to hear well in the darkness, and the quick footsteps and urgent whispering were as clear a sign of danger to me as the sound of guns and screams in a village outside. I left the false tunnel and scurried bent over toward trapdoor 12. I know the tunnels so well, I don't have to feel my way, even when it's as dark as if my eyes were closed.

Had something happened to Bay? I was afraid to know, but I couldn't stay away. And it was only natural that people would come to help; no one would think it was strange that I was there now.

In the tunnel just below the trapdoor someone had a dim oil lamp. Dang and Tran were there, and the commander, and some other men. But where was Bay? I couldn't ask them about him directly. "Are you okay?" I whispered to Tran. "What—"

And then Bay jumped lightly in through the trapdoor. He didn't say a word. He stepped back and pulled the cover off the booby trap. Bright light splashed down from an enemy flashlight; there were enemy voices. And then down came an enemy soldier, a small one. He didn't have trouble squeezing through the trapdoor. He fell easily down—and onto the sharp bamboo spikes in the uncovered pit directly underneath.

In the light of the flashlight from above, Bay silently slit the enemy's throat before he could even scream. "Detonate now! Hurry!" he whispered. He didn't turn and look at the commander or at me or at anyone. His eyes had adjusted to the light outside and he'd be blind inside the tunnel now.

Another enemy soldier was shouting outside the tunnel. Now they would know about trapdoor 12. We'd have to run from this section of the tunnels and abandon it for the enemy to discover and try to destroy. And I had worked for so many weeks on my secret project! But that was a selfish thought. I stifled my disappointment.

Bay pulled himself up through the trapdoor just as the commander pushed the detonator. The bombs went off outside, and the tunnels shook, and earth spilled down. And then the top half of a dead enemy soldier was hanging down inside the trapdoor; Bay must have killed him while he was distracted by the helicopters blowing up. He was bigger and fatter than the other one. He was stuck, blocking the entrance. If we couldn't get him out of there, and Bay couldn't get through, he'd be captured. No one had to say it. We tugged at the enemy's arms. He was really wedged in there.

And then there was a shower of earth from the trapdoor and he came tumbling through, onto the body of his companion. Bay came after him, standing on the bodies as he snugly fitted trapdoor 12 back in place above him.

He stumbled off the bodies and crouched against the wall. "It's okay," he whispered, breathing hard. "Those were the only two who saw us. The rest won't have any idea how we got in."

"Good work," the commander said. "With your cell, it's always good work, Bay," he added. He rarely said anything so complimentary to anyone.

I went over to pick up some of the M-14s that had not yet

been carried to the storage room down below. A pile of them was right next to Bay's feet, and as I bent over I whispered to him, "Bay. I have a surprise. Come to the false tunnel." I hoped no one heard me. I picked up the guns and hurried away.

And then, in the small room I had made in the curving false tunnel, I waited. It would take a while for Bay and Dang and Tran to describe the layout of the camp to the commander and the secretary, who would write it all down.

Bay and Dang and Tran are an elite cell. That means they have their own sleeping quarters, a rare privilege. And that was the other reason Bay chose Dang and Tran. He's known them all his life. They're women, and understand some things better than most of the men. They wouldn't report him if he sometimes spent unexplained time away from his cell—or even slept in another place. And now we had a place.

I heard his familiar step. I lit the candle. "Bay! In here!"

He could hardly believe I had dug a bedroom for us. He was astonished. He was also careful. "Nobody knows?" he said.

"Nobody. Dang and Tran won't be a problem, will they?"

"I told them I'd be away for a little while. They didn't ask any questions. And . . . Oh, to be able to sleep together!"

And then he cried. Bay can cry with me. "I couldn't do those things if I didn't have you to come back to," he said.

And we lay there in each other's arms, listening to the shouting Americans running back and forth above us as the sun came up outside.

WILLIAM SLEATOR

The Vietnamese people won.

I visited the Cu Chi tunnels in Vietnam—as a tourist—in October 1992. There isn't a lot left of them; large portions of the tunnels were finally destroyed by carpet bombing. But you can still crawl down into underground meeting rooms and dormitories with hammocks, and see the kitchen and an operating room (which has a case of medical equipment, including a saw). It was a very intense and moving experience.

Back in this country I did a lot of research. I read *The Tunnels of Cu Chi* by Tom Mangold and John Penycate. There is also a shorter book called *Tunnel Warfare*, for younger people and with more photographs, by the same authors. It is part of a series, *The Illustrated History of the Vietnam War*. I recommend these books to readers interested in finding out more.

I am now working on my twentieth book. The most important award to me is the one *Interstellar Pig* won: the California Young Readers' Medal, which is voted for by students. My most recently published book, as I write this, is *Oddballs*, which is a collection of crazy stories about my own childhood. I divide my time between Bangkok, Thailand, and Boston, Massachusetts.

DANCING
BACKWARDS

by Marion Dane Bauer

For Annie

I suppose I could have known about myself when I was four years old. About being different from the other little girls, I mean. That was the year Miss Reinhardt's "baby" ballet class performed for the Women's Club in my hometown.

I was a sunbeam. We were all sunbeams. There must have been ten of us in the class. Our costumes—I can see them even now, fifty years later, as clearly as I can see the well-worn sweats I have on today—were yellow satin. With little puffed sleeves and short pleated skirts and matching panties.

I used to love dresses with matching panties. I could twirl or turn somersaults or just stand around holding my skirt up and watch the neighborhood boys gog. Until my brother told on me and my mother said, crossly, that even if the panties matched, I wasn't to let anyone see. I couldn't figure that. What was the point of matching panties if they were supposed to be kept hidden?

But it wasn't the costume—or even the panties—that made the recital memorable. I'm sure I must have looked like every other sunbeam that day. At least I did until we began to dance.

We were supposed to sashay in, a kind of sideward sliding step, facing the audience. Only standing in the small room, shut off from the main one by a curtained doorway, I couldn't figure out where the audience was going to be, which way *they* would be facing.

I even left my place in the line of little girls and peeked past the curtain a couple of times to locate the rows of faces. Ah, yes. There they were. But the moment I stepped back into line, I would forget all over again. Were they on this side of the room or that? Sometimes in my life I have been sure I knew something when, really, I didn't have a clue, but this wasn't one of those times. I was perfectly clear about the fact that I was confused. So finally, I did the best I could. I chose a direction, crossed my fingers, and waited for the first notes from the piano, my entire body vibrating with anticipation.

When the music sounded, all the little girls sashayed into the next room, smiling brightly at the audience as we had been taught. Except for me. I sashayed in, all right, and I smiled, too, but I found myself smiling at a blank wall.

The audience began to titter, and then the titters turned into laughs. I knew, of course, that the entire Women's Club—including, I presumed, my very own mother—was laughing at me. I even knew that they thought my mistake was "cute." And I found them exceedingly rude.

But despite the laughter, perhaps even because of it, I couldn't turn around. I had these steps to do, you see, and if I turned around, I'd mess up. So I did the whole dance—did everything the other girls did, and did it as well as they did, too—with my back to the audience.

When it came time to bow, I turned around at last. Which made all the women laugh even harder. But there was space to do it then without spoiling the dance. I scowled over my curtsy to send the laughing women a message about their rudeness, but I suppose they found that "cute," too.

Later, on our way home, my mother asked me a question in her most subdued, most carefully considered voice. "Thea," she said, "why didn't you just check out the other little girls before you came on? You could have faced the same way they were." And you know, I didn't have an answer. I still don't. Except that it had never occurred to me to check anything except my own inner sense of direction. Not once. Even when I knew my inner sense of direction was confused.

The day Cindy and I got thrown out of St. Mary's Academy for Young Women, I remembered, for the first time in many years, my backwards dance. And do you want to know something? I laughed. I realized then that if I'd stayed as true to myself at seventeen as I'd been when I was four, I wouldn't have needed Sister Stephen Marie to tell me who I was.

But then, I shouldn't refer to the incident in so cavalier a fashion. One wasn't *thrown out* of St. Mary's Academy for Young Women, of course. This was 1956, and the nuns did nothing so crude as to throw anyone anywhere. Cindy and I were merely asked, politely, to leave. Girls like us, we were told, were a danger to other students. For all I know, we were a danger to the sisters and to the aging band of spinster teachers as well.

I can still feel the chill that crawled up my spine when we were called out of literature class. We were studying a play, I forget which one, by that charming old queer Oscar Wilde. Only nobody said he was queer, of course. He was a play-wright, an *artiste*! Whatever they thought of queers, St. Mary's Academy for Young Women was high on *artistes*.

Miss Brown, Sister SM's righthand woman, stepped into the classroom. "Thea Evans and Cynthia O'Connell are to come with me to Sister Stephen Marie's office," she said. "Immediately." And the class, even Sister Mary Ruth, our teacher, drew in a communal breath. No one was ever called to Sister Stephen Marie's office except for grave cause.

Miss Brown, delivering the message, confirmed the seri-ousness of our predicament by looking over her glasses from one of us to the other and smacking her thin, blue lips. It was, everyone knew, the deepest satisfaction of that woman's life to see girls brought before the principal in disgrace.

Without a word, without taking time, even, to gather our books, we followed Miss Brown down the echoing stone hall-way, our shoulders bumping softly now and then. For a skinny woman Miss Brown had a walk that was muscular and swift, which left us hurrying after her, not daring so much as a glance in each other's direction. We both knew, of course. And yet—and this is true—we didn't have the slightest clue.

"Sit down," Sister Stephen Marie said when we presented ourselves at the door of her cave. "No," she added, when we proceeded, innocently, to companion chairs side by side against the wall. "You . . . there." She indicated the already-chosen chair for Cindy. "And you"—she nodded curtly at me—"over there."

Cindy sat down, and I moved to the distant chair, already feeling the sting of our separation. Cindy was my roommate, my best friend, a girl whose large, nearsighted, spectacularly blue eyes produced copious tears in sad movies—or just if she got too tired—and I always felt that it was my responsibility to protect her from the world.

Miss Brown had taken up a position at the door, like a prison guard, blocking the exit.

We were good girls, Cindy and I. Good students, too. As good as any at St. Mary's Academy, and everyone in that room knew it. I also knew, and I'm sure Cindy did too, that being "good" wasn't going to save us. There was a long silence in which the very air in the room seemed to grow thin, as though we were gradually being deprived of oxygen.

Sister SM spoke at last. "Perhaps," she said—her wimple pinched her soft, round face into a frown—"you girls would like to explain these." And she held up two valentines, the gaudiest, the laciest, the mushiest we had been able to find. One was addressed to Cindy from me, the other to me from Cindy.

I looked across at Cindy and saw the heat mottling her cheeks. Behind her glasses tears were beginning to pool.

"It was a joke," I said, quickly. It didn't even occur to me to wonder how the cards had come to Sister's attention. They had been stuck up on the bulletin board in our room. I chattered on. "Lots of the other girls were getting valentines from home. From boyfriends. Don't you see?" Sister SM waited. Her eyes were blue, too, but as pale as ice, as though years of prayer—or of facing down errant girls—had drained all their color away. It was obvious that those eyes didn't *see* anything. "And so we sent them to one another. Just . . ."

I was running out of breath. It was beginning to dawn on me what terrible thing we were being accused of. I had heard of lesbians, of course. Fairies, they were called. If you wore yellow on a Thursday, you were a fairy. Or green. And though I was seventeen years old, that was the sum total of what I knew. (I *never* wore yellow or green on Thursdays. Cindy was careful too.)

"Just for fun," Cindy said, coming to my rescue. "We bought the cards just for fun."

"They were so corny, you see," I added, desperation pushing my voice high. "We thought they were funny."

"And neither of you has a boyfriend at home to send you valentines?" Miss Brown spoke from behind us. She made it sound like some kind of crime, not having a boyfriend to send valentines from home.

"No," I said, and I wanted to add, "Do you?" But of course, I knew better than that. Instead I stumbled on, almost equally unwisely, to say, "Who needs them? Boys are so—"

"Uncouth." Cindy filled in the word for me. We had a habit of that. Completing one another's sentences.

You would think a statement like that, denigrating boys, would please a nun, at least the nuns I knew in 1956. After all, that's why girls were sent to St. Mary's Academy, to keep us away from boys. And the sisters had always taken their responsibility in that regard very seriously. It was partly because Cindy and I had little inclination to run off to town to meet the local hoods that we'd always had a reputation for being "good." But Sister SM's face just pinched harder. She was beginning to look like someone had gathered a thread through her lips and pulled it tight.

Miss Brown moved forward to stand next to Sister's desk now. "And what about," she demanded to know, "your beds?"

"Our beds?" Cindy and I wondered in the same breath. Had we forgotten to make them that morning?

Sister Stephen Marie shook her hands out of her voluminous sleeves, clasped them, and leaned forward across her desk as though this discussion about our beds were going to be the most interesting part of her day. "A sink overflowed this morning, directly above your room," she explained in a low, almost conspiratorial voice. "Miss Brown, when she was attending to the matter, stepped into your room to make sure there was no damage below."

"Was there?" I asked stupidly. I still didn't get it. What was wrong with our beds?

Miss Brown's lips were parted and her teeth gleamed. "Why are your beds pushed together?" she demanded to know. "Why haven't you left them on the opposite sides of the room, where they belong?"

Why? My glance slid to Cindy. She was staring at the floor.

I realized instantly that the two of us couldn't have looked more guilty if we'd been caught in the very act we were being accused of. "We just like to . . . talk," I said, weakly. But even to my own ears the answer didn't convince.

"Talk?" Sister SM demanded. "You have to have your beds right up close like that, not an inch of space between them, just to talk?"

It was then that Cindy straightened her back, lifted her chin, and ended the interrogation. "When we're going to sleep, we like to lie close together," she said. She spoke matter-of-factly, as though it were as innocent a practice as, indeed, it was. "Like spoons, you know?"

The room quivered with silence. My little Cindy! My mouse! I'd never felt prouder of her or loved her more than at that moment, sitting there with her back poker straight and her eyes dry, bringing our time at St. Mary's Academy for Young Women to a close.

Frankly, I couldn't tell if she didn't get it, what we were being accused of, or if she understood perfectly and didn't care. But either way I was on her side, because she was telling the truth. Our truth. We did like to lie together in the damp cool of that old dormitory. We even liked to wrap our arms around one another. Just that. Just strong arms enclosing, warm breath tickling the back of the neck, the flannel of our pajamas clinging like those old Sunday-school flannel boards. Once, we had even turned around and faced one another . . . and kissed. But it had been such a startling experience that we'd never done it again.

"Are you—" Sister Stephen Marie said, and before she could finish what she'd begun, I'd leaped to my feet and shouted, "NO!"

"No?" she repeated, her pale eyebrows disappearing behind the pleated fabric of her wimple. And somehow her question, though quieter, was more forceful than my shout. "How did you know what I was going to ask, Thea?"

"How could I not know?" I asked, and to my surprise, I was the one who was crying. Cindy still sat there, perfectly calm, while the tears poured down my face. I wanted to add, *You've got a dirty mind, Sister. Both of you've got dirty minds!* But I was too well brought up to say anything like that.

And besides, something else was going on for me, something that pushed all the rest aside, even my desire to graduate from St. Mary's Academy, which was going to be an entree to the private college my parents had picked out.

Cindy and I were being accused of an act we never would have dared commit, one I sincerely believe that neither of us had even imagined until that moment. But if we could be accused, then it meant, suddenly, that such a thing was possible in a way it had never been before. For the first time in my life I saw that the love, the actual, corporeal love, of another woman was something to be desired, that it might even be more to be desired than the approval of nuns and teachers and parents. Than entrance to a private college. Than the good opinion of the entire world, for that matter. I was stunned and frightened . . . and filled with the most incredible joy.

The rest of the "interview" went quickly. Our parents were

called, told the horrendous news. Their daughters were . . . Well, perhaps if we were supervised closely, kept from further contact, we might yet turn out all right. But in the meantime St. Mary's Academy for Young Women could not risk . . .

I have forgotten most of the details. Intentionally, I suppose. I only begin to remember clearly from the moment when, sent to pack, Cindy and I stood, for the last time, in the room we had shared for so many innocent, so many lost months.

Cindy must have made the same discovery as I in the same manner as I, because when I turned to look at her, her face had a kind of luminescence I had never seen before. Truly, she looked like one of the angels in the stained-glass windows of the school chapel. Neither of us spoke, but after a timeless moment when the terror and the ecstasy vibrated between us like the strings of that same angel's harp, we stepped into one another's arms and kissed, long and sweetly. At that moment neither of us remembered, neither of us cared, that at St. Mary's Academy for Young Women doors were allowed no locks.

When we finally broke our embrace, it was Cindy, my precious Cindy, who, with awkward, trembling hands, began to unbutton my blouse. And then the discoveries—the warm silk of skin, the mound of breast and pubis, the deep, deep communion—began.

MARION DANE BAUER

I have published thirteen books for young people, including *On My Honor*, a 1987 Newbery Honor Book; *What's Your Story? A Young Person's Guide to Writing Fiction*, a 1993 ALA Notable Book; and my most recent, *A Question of Trust*.

"Dancing Backwards" is entirely true and mostly made up. I did dance backwards when I was four years old and the audience did laugh. Only very recently has it occurred to me that I could have checked the "normalcy" of my position by merely looking at the other little girls, but it tells me something important about myself that I didn't.

I never attended an academy for young women. I was a counselor for an Episcopal Church girls' camp, though, and I and the young woman I loved—two of the best counselors the sisters had—were not invited back after that summer. We were as innocent in our love as two young women could be, and we were never even able to bring ourselves to speak of the reason our services would no longer be required, though we both understood. We never discovered the full sweetness possible between us, either.

She married a year later, at eighteen. I followed the same path soon after. (It is true that we were *good* girls.) And it wasn't until thirty years later that I finally recognized what direction it was I had been facing, all along.

When I was four years old I understood what it has taken me all these years to discover. It's not the audience's perspective that matters, or their applause. It's the dance.